Operation Cleanup

Megan F. Beach

Introduction

I desperately struggled to move as the shots got closer and louder. I felt frozen, stuck. My hearing slowly faded to a buzzing and then nothing.

It's over.

That simple thought, two clear words, sent chills throughout my body. I stopped moving and accepted my approaching death. Memories of loved ones rushed into my mind, my heart aching to hug them one last time. A deep sadness consumed me as I realized I would never achieve my dream of becoming a published author. I specifically thought about the first manuscript I ever completed, a story about a group of teens trying to survive a dystopian post-nuclear world. As the shooter approached where I lay injured, my dream of sharing that story with the world slipped away and I braced myself for the end.

I made it out of that room alive, but two of my classmates — Reed Parlier and Riley Howell — did not. Their lives and dreams were stolen from them in those fatal moments that felt like an eternity. Reed's dream of developing video games and Riley's dream of serving his country came to a halt through no fault of their own. All the plans and hopes they had shattered as loud bangs, blood, and death forever changed our classroom.

I survived that day and since have actively pursued my dreams. Eventually, I published my work. But Reed and Riley will never get to live out their dreams, and that is a sobering reality I think about often.

As I consider why I continue to write despite many ups and downs, I remember them. Their memories, which inspire me to keep going even through hardship, made me decide I would dedicate a book to each of them. In those books, I incorporated aspects of their personalities and added in references to them. After realizing how much of Reed was present in early drafts of *Operation Cleanup*, I knew instantly this book was for him.

I began to include more of Reed's personality and interests into rounds of edits. Throughout these chapters are both hidden and obvious references to him, such as butterflies, the color green (our school color), the color orange (the color used for gun violence awareness), Elliot's love for technology, and so on. Elliot in particular became a character I associated with Reed due to his fascination with technology, his habit of wearing only one sock at times, his kind personality, and his outward appearance resembling Reed's.

All of this was my attempt to capture a picture of who Reed was, my sweet friend whose dreams for his future were cut short due to an act of gun violence. I did not get the chance to say goodbye to Reed in those scary moments, so I made sure Elliot was able to hear everything I wish I could've said. Saying goodbye in a bloody classroom torn apart by an active shooter was not possible for us, but I knew I could make it work for Oliver and Elliot. I only pray that somehow and somewhere, Reed heard.

It is also my prayer that just as my characters did not forget those lost in the final battle, the world may not forget Reed. This book is part of my effort to keep his memory alive, to ensure he is not lost in the growing pile of gun violence data. I hope my book reminds the world that he was here; a unique individual with his own hopes, quirks, and dreams.

I pray you see Reed's personality shining brightly through this book. His memory inspires me every day and I hope you will draw your own inspiration from this story, whether that is to be kinder, stronger, or bolder to shape a world where all of God's children are able to survive, thrive, and coexist in safety and harmony. Our differences don't have to divide us; they can unite us, especially when faced with a common oppressor. A better world is possible; we just have to have the courage to fight for it — the same courage Reed and Riley bravely displayed the day they lost their lives.

Don't let their stories die, and do not let the stories within you die, either. Live each day to the fullest and pursue your dreams wholeheartedly. Be bold, be kind, and be you.

We may never get the chance to do so again.

Life is hevel.

— Megan F. Beach

Chapter One

"Oliver!"

I scrunched my face as warm breath blew into my ear. Tugging on my bed sheets, I pulled them tightly around me and covered my face. I was exhausted after a long night of chit-chatting with my twin sister long past our bedtime. Tightening my grip on the sheets, I covered the top of my head as well. All I wanted was to drift back into my slumber.

"Please just let me have five more minutes!"

"Ollie, come on!" Fingers poked and tugged at my bed sheets. Rolling over, I did my best to ignore it all. "We have to go *now*!" Gentle finger pokes evolved into my whole body being shaken.

Inhaling sharply, I flung the sheets off and glared at my twin sister who stood at the edge of my bed. Her appearance was unkempt, something rather unusual for her. Her clothes hung off her slender frame and her hair was messy. She watched intently as I got up, running her hands through her thick blond hair as if to comb it.

"Olivia, what's happening?" I rushed to my dresser. *Something's wrong*, I thought as I shuffled through my clothes. Olivia never woke me up like this nor did she ever let her appearance get so rough. She was tidy and neat; from her side of the room, to her hair that she often decorated with braids, to how she dressed.

"I . . . I think the government has found out!" Olivia blurted out as I yanked some clothes from my dresser. She spun around so I could change out of my pajamas. "Regulators are all over the driveway. I got up here as fast as I could, but to think they've found out . . ."

I quickly pulled on a white tank top and tan cargo shorts, her words echoing through my mind as I slipped on my sturdy boots. *Not regulators!* I shivered, grabbing my pocket Bible and cross necklace and stuffing them into my pockets. I wasn't about to face anything — certainly not regulators — without either.

I turned around to find my sister on the floor, her knees pulled into her chest and her arms wrapped tightly around her legs. Tears glistened in the corners of her eyes, and she shook slightly. She blinked the tears away as I slowly crouched down next to her.

"Liv, it's going to be okay." Although my words were strong and steady, I wasn't so sure. Things could get ugly fast. Despite never coming face to face with regulators, Olivia and I had learned all about the harsh world they ruled outside our cozy orphanage, an orphanage that despised their cruel rules. I breathed in deeply, doing everything I could to settle my racing heart.

Olivia pulled me into a hug as she sobbed quietly. I squeezed my eyes shut, attempting to stop my own tears. The last thing I wanted was to appear cowardly or weak. *I have to be strong!* I reminded myself. *I need to be strong!* I took a few more big breaths, shaking away thoughts of regulators bursting down our bedroom door and dragging us away.

"Are you ready?" I asked, pulling away as she stopped shaking. I couldn't bear the thought of rushing her. After all, she never rushed me. Yet I knew this moment was different. There wasn't a second to spare. *I'm sorry,* I apologized silently as I climbed to my feet. *But we have to get moving.*

Olivia started to get up, only to crash to the ground as loud bangs and screams echoed from the floor below us. I glanced around our small bedroom, my heart jumping into my throat. Everything suddenly felt so uncanny despite this small room being our safe place for years. Even our stacks of old toys, books, and other belongings scattered about now felt foreign.

My thoughts raced to my friend Caleb who lived on the ground floor. My pulse began to ring in my ears as I pictured him and the others being beaten and dragged away by the regulators. *Please, Lord, let him be okay!*

Olivia tugged my arm. "Oliver, we have to go now!" I remained quiet, only offering a small nod in response as she pulled me to the window.

The window gave way with no struggle. Unhooking the lock and placing her hands along the glass, Olivia slid the panes up. A warm breeze stirred into the room, serving as an unpleasant reminder of the outside world that awaited us.

I shifted closer, peering out into the world below. Across the grassy field that functioned as the orphanage's backyard stood a dense forest. I squinted, seeing no end to it. The trees were dark and looming, but I had no doubt we could handle whatever they held.

"Do you want to jump together?" I whispered. I did my best to focus despite the sound of yells from farther down our hall.

"It's not big enough for the both of us, silly," Olivia scoffed as she climbed onto the windowsill. She pulled her legs up, swinging them around so they dangled freely outside. I felt a bit of surprise when she didn't jump immediately. Olivia liked to accomplish tasks quickly and often did so with ease. She never procrastinated and I couldn't understand why she appeared to now given our current circumstances.

"It's only a small quick jump, Olivia," I said, hoping to reassure her in case her hesitation was due to nerves. "You'll be fine." I struggled to remain calm as more shouts split through the air. If regulators did happen to burst through our door, I decided I would quickly push her out then jump myself.

My sister tilted her head back, glancing around our shared room. "Goodbye," she whispered, her eyes glistening with tears. She took in a deep breath then pushed herself off the sill. Relief rushed over me as she landed safely on the grass below.

Okay, Oliver, I thought, climbing onto the sill. *It's your turn now. Just one small fall, or rather, one tiny jump to safety.* Even though we were only on the second floor, the ground below now seemed so far away. Olivia glanced up with wide eyes, taking a few steps back to give me ample space. As I braced myself for the fall, I heard loud voices outside our bedroom door. Thinking fast, I grabbed the window frame and pulled it shut as I leaped.

Almost as soon as I hit the ground, Olivia took hold of my arm and yanked me toward the trees. I staggered to my feet, glancing back to discover my plan to close the window had been successful. *Yes!* Hopefully the regulators would assume from the closed window and empty room that no one occupied it. Hopefully they wouldn't even bother searching through it and our escape would go unnoticed.

My moment of satisfaction was cut short as ear-piercing screams rang from around the orphanage. I did everything I could to resist crying as my sister pulled me farther away from our home, from the perfect room we had decorated to be our own. That room was our safe haven through the years, and now it was all gone.

"Oliver, quick!" My sister released her hold on me as we entered the trees. I cast one final glance back at the orphanage before dashing after her. Trees blurred past my vision as we ran on, eager to get away from the orphanage as the screams replayed in my mind.

Shaking my thoughts clear, I focused all my attention on getting through the thick forest. We leaped over old tree stumps and struggled past clumps of weeds. Thankfully, the tall trees offered some shade from the rising sun. As I caught Olivia's gaze, I saw my own worry and uncertainty reflected in her eyes. *We're going to be okay*, I silently promised her. *I won't let anyone hurt us.*

The strong rays of the sun lit the path as we raced on. My heart sank at the thought of having to face the hot day ahead without any fans or air conditioning. I was thankful for the shade we had now, but I wondered how much it would help in the coming hours.

Before long, the sun had reached the center of the sky. I swallowed, my throat absolutely parched. My heart raced along with my feet. I looked around as we pressed on into the forest, not sure what kinds of things were hiding among the trees. Focusing my thoughts elsewhere, I cast my gaze forward again. My heart was the heaviest it had ever been.

We were about to enter a living nightmare.

Chapter Two

After running for what felt like an eternity, Olivia and I took a small break at a creek. I stooped down, cupping my hands to take a drink from the rushing current. Although I hated the government, I was thankful for their commitment to ensuring the remaining water supply was safe for human consumption. The constant checking for radiation plus artificial filtration systems did pose the possibility of patrolling regulators, so I kept my eyes peeled for potential trouble and steadied my breath to be as quiet as possible.

Birds! My heart fluttered at the sound. I loved listening to birdsong. I could still remember the first time I heard them after emerging from the orphanage's bunker. That had been a glorious day following our tenth birthday. It was so exciting to experience the surface, to roll in the grass, and to gaze at the moon and the stars. I had never imagined things that appear so tiny could shine so bright.

The one thing I never looked forward to dealing with, the sun, now glared overhead. Thankfully, its heat was blocked by the trees that stretched far above our heads. The day had warmed up significantly, so much to the point I splashed some of the water onto my face and neck.

"Hey!" Olivia called out. She tugged at her shirt, which now had a water stain outlining its flower prints. "You're getting me all wet!"

I chuckled, splashing even more at her. "How about a 'thank you Oliver for cooling me off,' hm?" I sat down next to her after deciding I had tossed enough water in her direction.

"Never!" She grunted, tracing the water with her fingertips. She narrowed her eyes at me, and I instantly caught on to what she was planning.

"Go on, splash me!" I smirked. "I don't mind. I'm already soaked!"

Water smacked me in the face almost as soon as the words left me. Olivia sat up straight, looking quite pleased with herself.

"Guess we're even now," I said, glancing around as she drank from the stream. We had never actually explored the forest before since the adults back at the orphanage considered it too dangerous. The more I looked around, the more enchanted I was by our rest stop. The green moss and small vegetation covering the ground was vibrant, as were the wildflowers that poked out here and there. The sound of birds and other small critters, combined with the shade from the trees and the gentle whoosh of the water, created a lovely oasis in the thick forest. *Such a peaceful area*, I thought, still taking it all in.

But I knew this moment would not last. For the first time ever, we were completely on our own. Not only did we have to find food and shelter, but it was also vital we steer clear of any regulators. The run back at the orphanage had been too close — it was unlikely we could pull off another escape like that again. Regulators moved fast and the city we were approaching was full of the bastards. *How many will we come across? Would they really hurt us and take us away like in the stories everyone tells? Would they show any kind of mercy?* I shivered, shaking away the uncertainty and inching closer to my sister. I felt sure that as long as we stuck together, we would be alright.

"Look!" she said, pointing to a butterfly fluttering toward us.

"That's huge!" I smiled as it flapped its wings above the creek. "Looks like a peacock butterfly." My smile dropped as the creature landed on the water's surface. Olivia instantly reached out as it struggled against the current.

"Quick, Olivia! I don't think they can swim!"

In a flash, she scooped up the butterfly and placed it gently on the grass between us. We frantically fanned the creature with our hands, hoping our movements would dry its stunning orange and brown wings. Eventually the butterfly flapped its wings and flew off, both of us still mesmerized by it.

"She was so pretty!" Olivia exclaimed. "I hope we find more animals."

"Me too." I glanced over at my sister to find her committing her worst habit: biting her nails. "You *know* you're not supposed to do that." I let out a mild chuckle, thinking about how stern some adults at the orphanage were about it.

My sister smiled back, eventually dropping her hand and climbing to her feet. "Anyways, I'm ready whenever you are. You think we should continue the way we've been going?"

I took a few more deep breaths before standing up. "Yeah, that should take us to the city."

I observed my sister as I spoke. She still looked worn out. I couldn't help but wonder how well she had slept and felt regret for keeping her up so late. *Please Lord*, I silently prayed. *Let us get somewhere safe soon.*

With a quick leap, I crossed the creek. Olivia followed closely as I led this time. We traveled a bit slower than previously, looking around constantly for other humans. Occasionally, we spotted a few small creatures moving among the ground vegetation. Each made Olivia jump with an enthusiastic squeal.

"How much farther do you think the forest goes?" Olivia asked as we weaved around some trees covered with thick moss.

"I'm not sure," I said, amazed we were still in the forest after all this time. I never would have guessed it stretched so far from the nights I had stared into it from my window, imagining what secrets and mysteries it might hold.

"Don't you think we will look suspicious walking around the city?"

"Nah. It's a big population; I think somewhere around thirty thousand? Besides, how will they know we are unworthies? After all, we aren't even identical!"

My words were true, but Olivia and I still highly resembled each other. We both were pale with dark blue eyes, a small button nose, a slender frame, and dirty blond hair. Olivia's flowed in a naturally wavy pattern that rested right below her shoulders while mine curled just above my ears. People often assumed we were siblings, but no one guessed we were twins until we told them. I was confident no regulator would think we were twins.

Olivia did not ask any more questions as we continued our journey. We walked through the trees, jumping over fallen ones along the way. At one point our path was blocked by a huge fallen tree. Olivia attempted to balance perfectly on it, one foot at a time, which made both of us laugh as she failed each attempt. I gave it a try myself but was even worse. *So glad we can still have fun,* I thought with a smile, leaping off the log to follow my sister through the trees once more.

The sun continued crossing the sky as we marched on. It didn't take long for our shirts to completely dry. Birds chirped while they went about their daily lives, completely oblivious to the horrors happening in the human world. The familiar noise reminded me of the pet parakeets kept in the common room back at the orphanage. *Was anyone there to look after them now? What unfolded after we left?* Possibilities flashed through my mind: regulators shooting those they instantly deemed as unworthy, interrogating folks before tossing them into their cars, all while proclaiming they were only doing their 'God-given' duty of cleansing the Earth . . .

A loud horn interrupted my thoughts. Olivia and I froze then turned to each other. From the excitement in her eyes, I could tell we were thinking the same thing. Taking off in a run, we flew through the rest of the forest. We were a bit loud but neither of us cared.

"Yes!" I shouted with joy as we exited the forest into a large, overgrown field that sloped down into a road leading to a neighborhood. Beyond that stood the city which was a lot larger than I had imagined. Rows of houses faced us directly, with bigger buildings behind them. A bit farther were giant buildings, taller than anything I had ever seen. *Those must be skyscrapers*, I thought, recalling the stories from those who had ventured into the city. Beyond the cluster of tall buildings, I caught sight of smoke rising from factory towers, and off to the right appeared to be farmland that eventually sloped into lush mountains. The two of us admired the city as thousands within it continued about their daily routines.

I looked over at Olivia who returned my gaze. Her eyes glowed and a small smile lit up the rest of her round face. I returned a smile but instantly felt it drop as she suddenly took off.

"I'll race you!" she yelled as she started to jog through the thick grass. She slowed down briefly to look back at me.

"Hey!" I called out. "That's not fair, you got a head start!"

I took off after her as she sped up again. We easily crossed the field. I slowed down upon reaching the hill leading down into the city, which was a lot steeper than it appeared with its tough terrain. Dust and dirt crumbled beneath my feet as I landed next to my sister at the bottom of the hill. I burst into laughter, not even caring I lost the race.

"Beat you!" She nudged me through giggles. A bit more serious, she added, "You ready?" She stepped onto the paved road, her eyes scanning over the houses before meeting mine.

I returned her gaze. "Whenever you are."

Chapter Three

The two of us crossed the street quickly and entered the neighborhood. The houses were dark with boarded-up windows and roofs that caved in. Some even had broken furniture scattered on their front porches. All had overgrown lawns. Even the sidewalk was in rough shape as it crumbled beneath our feet. As I realized the area was deserted, I let my guard down. *We're safe*, I thought with a deep breath. *At least for now.*

"Ollie? No nukes dropped on us, right?" Olivia asked as we took in our first sight of the city.

"Not to my knowledge."

"Well, do you think this part of the city is abandoned?"

"Perhaps. But there's always a chance people are hiding out in these homes." The thought of people lurking behind the boarded-up windows made me shiver. With no one to guide us, it was uncertain who would be good and who might try to hurt us in the hope we had money or supplies.

"How long do you think this area has been this way?" Olivia asked, jumping over a hole in the sidewalk.

"I'm not sure, Liv," I said, sighing deeply. "I don't know any more than you do."

She sighed back. "No one at the orphanage said the city was abandoned like this."

"Oh, there's people. Just not in this area." They hadn't told us much about the city, but a few of the adults traveled to it from time to time, bringing back food and supplies. There had to be people somewhere.

"*No!*" Olivia's cry startled me. I raced to her side as she dropped down beside a dead animal. It was barely recognizable as a cat through the decay.

I slapped her hand back before she could touch it. "Don't!"

"Poor thing! I wonder how she died."

"Probably heat and lack of food," I said as I got to my feet and took a few steps forward. "Come on, I don't want to end up like that. We need to keep moving and find our own food and shelter."

Olivia ignored me. "I'm sorry little guy," she said softly, leaning closer to the dead cat. She glanced at it for a few more seconds before climbing to her feet, stepping carefully over it after me.

"You don't think that was a sign, do you?" Olivia asked as we continued. "Ms. Betsy once told me black cats were a bad sign."

"I doubt it," I said, jumping over a fallen powerline. "There's probably hundreds of dead animals around here." Now that I thought about it, I realized we hadn't stumbled upon many animals. Birds of course were plentiful, and we had spotted a few rabbits and squirrels while in the forest, but we hadn't seen any large animals. It felt odd that the forest and these overgrown suburbs held so little life.

"Besides," I added. "Ms. Betsy's crazy. Don't listen to her."

Olivia giggled at my comment. As we walked on crumbling sidewalks and overgrown lawns, my thoughts drifted back to the orphanage. I wondered what had happened in the hours since we'd been gone, especially to those left behind. *Was Ms. Betsy even still alive? Were any of them?*

I sighed, shaking the thoughts away. Right now, we had to focus on navigating the city and finding shelter. I kept my eyes peeled for any sign of other people or worse, regulators.

As we turned a street corner, we arrived at what appeared to have once been retail stores. They were boarded-up as well with thick vegetation creeping up their walls. Despite some sounds in the distance, this area of the city was clearly abandoned. Even the air was absent of birdsong. *How far does the city go?* I wondered, my feet growing sore and my belly rumbling. *Please Lord, let us find food soon!*

My interest piqued as my gaze rested on an old building across the road. Although it was boarded-up like the rest of the area, one side had completely caved in. Inside, I spotted various colors: sharp red booths and polished wooden tables surrounded by a green, checkered wallpaper. A sign across the roof read 'fresh pizza' with an image of a pizza below the letters. I wondered just how glorious the sign must've looked all lit up against a dark, dreamy night.

"I want to check this out," I said, taking the first few steps to cross the street.

Olivia rushed to my side, grabbing my arm. "Wait! What if someone's in there?"

"Look around," I said as she gradually released her grip. "This place is *deserted*. It'll be fine."

Olivia didn't say anything else, and the two of us slowly entered the former restaurant.

Whoa, I thought as I took my first steps over the crumbled wall. It was like stepping into the past. The tables throughout the place shone with polish. Wooden chairs were tucked under the tables and a few highchairs surrounded a corner bar dazzled with colorful tiles. Soft, pastel light fixtures hung from the ceiling and in the corner opposite of us stood an old jukebox like the ones I had looked at in photographs back in the bunker. Next to the jukebox were two wooden doors, each with a restroom sign still strung up at the entrance. To the left of us stood a large wooden door. Despite an entire side of this building being completely destroyed, the rest of it was in perfect shape. It looked like people could have dined here yesterday.

"This place is gorgeous!" Olivia remarked as we took in the unique shapes and colors.

I took a few steps toward the wooden door, noticing a piece of paper taped to it. Getting closer, I yanked the paper off.

"What does it say?" Olivia asked, coming to my side.

"By order of the highest regulators and their officials," I read. "This pizzeria is to be closed immediately. Anyone aligning with unworthies will not be tolerated, and neither shall opposition to our mighty emperor. All operations are to cease at once."

Olivia grabbed the paper out of my hands. "Let me see!" She read on about how the owner fed unworthies leftover pizza after close. It had also come to light that the owner had made some not-so-nice comments about the emperor. As the note explained, his resistance had led to his imprisonment and the closing of his restaurant.

Olivia laid the paper on a nearby table, shaking her head. "This is all so scary. Can't even critique the government or try to reduce food waste . . ." She glanced away as her words trailed off.

"I know," I said, taking her hand. "But we're safe now. It doesn't look like any regulators are in the area." I slowly opened the door, eager to find out what awaited us. I hoped somewhere behind it would be the kitchen stocked with food. I was aching to discover if those who had been here last left anything behind.

"Come on!" I pulled Olivia into the large space behind the wooden door. "Let's see if we can find some food."

Chapter Four

The kitchen was twice the size of the dining room with multiple stainless-steel ovens, stoves, and sinks lining the space. Dozens of pots, pans, and other cookware hung from the ceiling. A small island stood at the center and across from us was a small, barely lit room that I assumed was once an office. All I could distinguish through the office windows and the propped open door was a single desk. A few steps away from the office was a second door that was dark and closed. As I took it all in, I could not find a single crumb. The place was tidy and spotless.

Olivia propped the door we had come through open to let some sunlight in. "Oliver, look!" She pointed in the direction of the closed door next to the office. "Perhaps that door over there leads to a pantry."

We swiftly crossed the kitchen. As we approached the office, I noticed it was the only part of the restaurant that appeared abandoned. Besides a desk and a knocked down chair, it was completely empty. We passed by quickly, pausing briefly in front of the closed door before Olivia reached for the handles.

"Please, oh *please* have food!" Olivia said as she pushed the door open.

We peered inside the small room that led to another room with a large, closed door. Lining the walls of this room were shelves that seemed to be made out of the same material as the kitchen appliances. The bottom shelves contained crates with gallons of water, the middle shelves held some large tin cans and various bags, and the top shelf was stacked to the ceiling with pizza boxes and disposable napkins.

"FOOD!!!" Olivia rushed to pick up a can. "It's tomatoes!" She smiled, holding it up so I could read the label.

I grinned as I noticed the rest of the cans contained food and the large bags were filled with more. Most of the cans were either tomatoes or tomato sauce, but a few were vegetables such as mushrooms and olives. The bags lining the shelves were filled with pre-made dough, flour, cheese, and salad mix. Everything looked delicious except for some of the lettuce which had wilted.

"Do you think there's more food behind here?" I asked, making my way through the small space to the other door. Olivia followed closely behind, clutching the can of tomatoes tightly to her chest.

This door was much heavier than the other doors. It reminded me of the large, heavy doors back in the underground bunker we grew up in. I had never been able to open those doors on my own, but thankfully I'd grown a bit since then. As I pulled the door open, we peeked into another small room that only had empty shelves.

"Doesn't look like it," Olivia said, poking her head into the dark space. As soon as she ducked back out, I closed the door.

"Oh well. We've got plenty to eat here!" I glanced at the food lining the shelves. "Do you see a can opener anywhere?" I pulled a bag of cheese closer, my stomach growling even louder. "Perhaps some scissors too, to get these bags open." I was *ready* to feast.

"I'll go look in the kitchen!" Olivia placed the can of tomatoes back with the rest before dashing out the pantry. As she searched the kitchen, I looked around the pantry. Other than the food and crates, the shelves were empty. The space wasn't as large as the rest of the restaurant, but there was still enough room for two people to move around comfortably.

"Got them!" Olivia re-entered the pantry, holding a can opener in one hand and large scissors in the other. She handed the scissors to me. I threw the bag of cheese over my shoulder and grabbed a bag of salad mix. With my other hand I took a water gallon out of the crates. Olivia scooped up her can of tomatoes along with a can of olives.

"Let's eat in the kitchen. It's too dark in here," I instructed, exiting the poorly lit pantry. The sun lit up the kitchen a lot better.

We decided to eat on the kitchen island as it provided the most counter space. After a short prayer of thanks, we quickly dug in. Although it wasn't exactly what I had in mind, our first lunch away from home would do for now.

"Too bad there's no assembled pizzas!" I joked after a few handfuls of cheese.

"That would be too easy!" Olivia said. "Plus, you add gross toppings to your pizzas."

"I do not!"

"Do too! Like who wants to eat pineapple on pizza?"

"It's *good!*"

Olivia rolled her eyes playfully. "If you say so." In a more serious tone, she added, "Do you need anything from the pantry? I'm going to get my own gallon of water. You backwash too much."

"You backwash more!" I scoffed between bites.

Olivia stirred to her feet, a smirk on her face. "I'm guessing you don't need anything, then?"

I shook my head. "Thanks though."

After Olivia returned with her own water, the two of us ate on in silence for a bit. As Olivia cast her gaze down between bites, I caught a hint of sadness lingering in her eyes.

"Liv? What's wrong?" I asked, grabbing a handful of olives.

She sighed. "Just thinking." Her voice was soft, but hardened as she continued. "I mean . . . this *feels* like an adventure, but like . . . we're all alone now! We're lucky to have stumbled upon this place but we don't have a bed, or any clothes, and we can't go downstairs to a homecooked meal anymore, or play with our friends, or . . . well, most things! It's scary, isn't it?"

Her words hit me in the gut. "You're right," I said after swallowing down the olives. "It can be scary to think about, but look at it this way. We found this place, and we found food. For right now, for today, we're okay. Let's just take it one day at a time."

Olivia nodded. "I just want us to be safe. Out here it's uncertain, and you know what will happen if the regulators find us. There's no guarantee—"

Her response was interrupted by the loud screech of tires outside. I dropped down, my heart racing. Peering around the edge of the island, I saw my sister hide behind the pantry door. I met her troubled gaze as the sound of a car zoomed past the pizzeria. Working cars were few and rare since the war. It wasn't like anyone could get their hands on them. The only people known to have access to them were regulators.

Realizing we had left the kitchen door open, I slowly crawled toward it. I moved forward on my knees and hands, praying no one would look into the pizzeria and spot me. My pulse rang in my ears and my limbs struggled to move forward. My vision narrowed as my sweaty palms moved closer and closer to the open door. I shook off cheese crumbs once I got closer, glancing over to see Olivia still crouched down, her eyes wide as she watched my every move.

I carefully climbed to my feet as I reached the door. The rest of the restaurant was still empty with sunlight shining through the open side to the right of me. From what I could perceive from my angle, the road was also vacant. I pushed the door closed about an inch at a time, hoping and praying the movement was not noticeable to the outside world.

I dropped back down to hide after the door creaked. Through the darkness, I spotted Olivia crawling toward me.

"See anything?" she whispered as she reached my side.

I shook my head. Olivia slowly rose to her feet but then quickly dropped back down as another car passed, siren sounding. A third car siren accompanied it, both eventually dying down as they got farther and farther away. I closed my eyes, attempting to steady my breath and racing heart. *Lord, are we safe here?* After a few moments of catching my breath, I felt a moment of certainty that everything was alright now. In my mind, I pictured the cars driving past so quickly they wouldn't have even noticed the half-open door. *They couldn't have possibly seen us with how fast they were going,* I reassured myself. *There's no way they saw us.*

Once I felt a bit steadier, I turned to my sister. "We need to be quieter and more careful. Those sounded a lot like how folks describe regulator cars. It's possible they still patrol around the area."

"But they wouldn't come in here, right?" Olivia asked, closing the kitchen door even more. She left it cracked just enough so we could see our surroundings.

"I wouldn't think so," I said, stirring to my feet. "But we can never be too certain."

"I can't imagine they'd care to explore an abandoned building."

I didn't respond as we slowly made our way back to the kitchen island to finish our lunch. Regardless of what the rest of the day held, I wanted to face it with a full belly.

Chapter Five

After we had eaten our fill, we headed out of the pizzeria into the unknown. Both of us stayed close to the abandoned shops, ready to duck into them in case any more cars zoomed past. Our time at the pizzeria had made us realize that although this part of the city appeared abandoned, it was unlikely to be completely vacant. After all, regulators wouldn't waste their time driving around empty streets.

How many others like us are out here? I wondered as we entered another worn down and lifeless neighborhood. The houses were boarded-up as well and some appeared to be in even worse condition than previous ones. Windows were shattered and graffiti covered the old brick houses. Porch railings had completely fallen down and pieces of broken furniture were scattered along the street. Although I knew no nukes had exploded over the city, one might mistakenly assume so due to the state of the neighborhoods.

"It's so hot! I miss our fan," Olivia whined as we continued down the sidewalk.

"Me too. But I am *not* making that trek back to the orphanage. I have no clue how to get back there anyways."

"Yeah, it wouldn't really be worth it. The regulators would have cleared it out by now." Olivia perked up a bit. "I hope they enjoy all my cute clothes."

I rolled my eyes. "I'm sure they'll *love* all the cat and flower prints."

"Better than your camouflage and basketball shorts."

"Hey! Don't hate on my style," I chuckled.

Olivia snickered. Her eyes narrowed as we reached the end of the abandoned street. "Oliver, look!" She pointed toward a working streetlight a few blocks away.

"Let's be careful," I whispered as we got closer. Reaching a part of the city that had electricity meant people, especially regulators, might be lurking around. The thought made me shudder. *Would those living in the city be friendly? Or were they all spies for the emperor and his regulators, waiting for the opportunity to turn people like Olivia and me in?* I prayed no one who spotted us would guess we were twins.

As we approached the streetlight, other lit ones came into view. The houses changed drastically, too. Some remained in the abandoned, worn-out state but others were shockingly well-maintained and beautiful. The porches were upkept with intact furniture and dazzling light shone through the windows. The houses were painted bright, vivid colors and all had beautiful green lawns. Some homes even had small trees and bushes out front. A few rose bushes stuck out among the vegetation and lots of sunflowers lined the sidewalks, which were solid and clean with no weeds poking through.

"Do you think this is how all homes looked before the war?" Olivia asked.

"I don't know." I wondered about the possibility myself. "It sure is beautiful, though."

The houses continued to look maintained as we ventured farther into the city. Eventually we came across other people, all of whom walked straight ahead with one foot landing perfectly in front of the other and their arms swinging just slightly as they moved. Most wore fancy suits and ties while others had pleated dresses on. Very few were dressed casually. They had stern, emotionless eyes that seemed to barely acknowledge our existence as we passed by, causing us to feel a bit more relaxed once we realized none of them seemed interested in reporting us to regulators. So far, all the people only had blond hair and blue eyes, regardless of skin color. I couldn't help but ponder how many of them used artificial dyes and contacts to achieve such a look. The striking similarity of those in the city intrigued me. Back at the orphanage we were all sorts of hair shades and eye colors. Here, everyone looked and even walked the same. Olivia and I exchanged a confused look. To better blend in, we attempted to walk like the city residents.

I glanced up in amazement as we entered the center of the city. The buildings here were massive, taller than anything I'd ever walked alongside before. They made our three-story orphanage look tiny. The skyscrapers were dazzling, made of various marbles and stones. Most were made of reflective windows. I couldn't help but glance over myself as we passed them, offering myself a small smile.

"Hey, Oliver?" Olivia called from a few steps ahead. "Can we take a break somewhere?"

"Sure." I felt certain we were safe. Not a single regulator had driven past since we started our journey into the city and none of the people paid us any attention. "Pick whichever building you think is best."

Olivia continued for a few more blocks then approached one of the smaller skyscrapers. I followed her through the set of doors, relieved by the cool air.

The building was like one massive hallway with little stores lining both sides. The white marble floors shone, and the bright overhead lights lit up the place. The space was crowded with people coming and going from one store to the next. The stores seemed to go on forever, and a large artificial pond ahead blocked our view of the other side. A few plants hung along the walls and an overhead speaker was running a loop, going from *Praise our mighty emperor for all his wonderful works* to *Become beautiful today! Pick up your dyes and contacts at Miller's, located between Dawn's Spa and Perdue's Cookware* to reports on the weather. From farther down the hall, I caught a whiff of freshly baked pretzels.

"Nice choice, Olivia!" Not a single regulator was in sight and I knew we could easily blend in with the crowd. The two of us strolled down the hallway, making sure we walked as upright and neatly as everyone else.

We passed clothing stores, jewelry stores, beauty stores, a few barber shops, a shoe polishing station, and a few food stands. The artificial pond was beautiful, with plants outlining it and a few pipes spraying up water every few seconds. It even contained fake rocks and lily pads, but unfortunately no fish. While it was pretty, the creek from the start of our day was far better. A few people sat alongside the pond, nodding and waving as we passed by. It was the most interaction we'd witnessed from those in the city.

"Let's check out this store." Olivia pulled me in the direction of what appeared to be a clothing store for teens. "We're going to need some new clothes now."

I pulled back right before entering the store, causing Olivia to turn around sharply. "How in the world are we going to pay?" I muttered under my breath just loud enough for Olivia to hear.

Olivia chuckled, reaching her hands into her pockets. She pulled out some green bills. "I'm already a step ahead of you! You think I'd leave unprepared? I grabbed as much as I could once I realized we had to leave the orphanage."

I smiled as we headed into the store. The place was a lot bigger than it appeared with hundreds of clothing racks covering the floor. I at once made my way to the basketball shorts while Olivia went off to some colorful shirts. After some time shuffling through the many racks, we each ended up with arms full of new shorts and shirts. We also grabbed bags of new underwear and socks. When it came time to check out, I was relieved to find out we had enough money. The cashier loaded our items into two large paper bags, one of which she handed to me and the other to Olivia.

"I think we have enough clothes now," Olivia said as we exited the store.

I nodded in agreement, my tummy grumbling. "How much money do we have left?"

Olivia reached into her pocket, taking out some coins and a couple crumbled up bills. "Two dollars and . . ." she trailed off briefly to count up the change. "Thirty-six cents!"

I glanced at the bakery close by, shock rising in me as I scanned over the menu. *Fifteen dollars for a small plain cookie?* I never would have guessed how expensive the world outside the orphanage truly was. We had shared just about everything we had, especially food. Large pots of stews and soup that combined whatever ingredients we had were constantly on the stove. Although the stews and soups became so bland to me after eating them for years, I was suddenly craving them.

"The day's ending. It would be dinner time back home," Olivia said as if reading my mind. Before I could say anything, she turned and started walking in the direction we had come from. I quickly caught up with her, my bag swinging as I moved my arms to mimic those around us. As full as it was, it surprisingly wasn't too heavy.

"Should we head back to that restaurant?" Olivia asked. I felt relieved that she chose to refer to the pizzeria as a "restaurant" instead of including specifics. I had no clue who might be listening to our conversation, and the cameras lining the ceiling of this building made me uneasy along with the loudspeaker spouting ads and praises for the emperor.

"I think that would be our safest bet," I said, realizing I also needed to be careful with my words. "But I'd like to get some dinner first."

"Most definitely!" Olivia said as we passed the fake pond. "I'm so hungry."

"Me too. Maybe . . ." I trailed off as an idea entered my mind. I wanted to wait until we were outside before sharing it.

"Maybe what?" Olivia asked, smiling at a group of young children we passed.

"Hold on," I muttered, pushing open the door and emerging into the hot and humid city air. Despite the sunset, the air was still bitterly warm. The streetlights were all lit, shining down different blues and oranges onto the street below.

"Maybe what?" Olivia repeated as we began to return the way we came.

"Maybe we could find some food around here?" I suggested.

Before I could explain further, Olivia chimed in. "And how are we going to get it? There's barely anything back at the restaurant and I barely have money left. We can't just steal!"

"I *know* and I didn't say we would steal." I took a deep breath. The last thing we needed right now was an argument. "Remember how the adults at the orphanage always complained about restaurants throwing out food? Come on," I glanced around quickly before ducking behind an alley lined with diners. "Let's search these dumpsters."

Olivia followed quietly. Along the alleyway were back doors and a few large dumpsters. I made my way to one, hoping and praying it would contain some edible food. Reaching as high as I could, I slowly and carefully slid the lid off. *Yes!* Among the rubbish was chicken tenders, lots of French fries, onion rings, pizza slices, sandwiches, and bags of chips. Most of the food looked completely untouched and sat on top of closed black bags. Olivia reached for some of the chicken tenders while I pulled out half a deli sub.

"Just make sure you look it over before eating," I instructed, opening the sandwich to inspect for teeth marks or mold. The deli slices, pickles, lettuce, and tomatoes looked remarkably fresh. I sunk my teeth in and quickly began to munch away.

Olivia reached back in, taking out more food. "Let's gather as much as we can to take back with us," she said between bites. "That way we can have even more back home."

Home. Her last word echoed through me. She had called the pizzeria *home.* As I swallowed some of the sandwich, I was hit with a wave of fear. *This really is our home now.* The orphanage was gone — there was no way we could ever return now that regulators had raided it. Strangely, I felt an odd sense of peace slowly replace the fear. *This is our home now. And we're going to make the best of it. And we're going to be just fine.*

I smiled, reaching in for more food to fill up my bag. "Sounds like a plan."

The two of us ate a few more bites before journeying back to the pizzeria, our bags filled to the brim and our bellies full.

***

"Do you remember the way home from here?" I asked, the sky darkened above us. Unlike my sister, who had a strong photographic memory, I was starting to feel lost as the streets began to look the same. We had exited the busy areas of town and entered the neighborhoods. The houses in this part of the city were well-maintained with neatly trimmed yards and small vegetation lining the driveways. The setting sun shone on the homes, giving them a golden glow. My bag swung at my side as we walked on the even and clean sidewalk.

"Of course I do!" Olivia straightened up with a spring in her step. "We need to turn right at this upcoming intersection, then cut through a few more streets, then back to our abandoned one!"

"Lead the way."

The two of us continued in silence for a bit. I glanced around, studying the area so I could remember it for future reference. *I'll have to learn at least some of the route*, I decided. It wouldn't be fair to Olivia if I didn't at least try.

Olivia shifted closer to me suddenly. "Ollie," she whispered. "Where do you think all those people are going?"

I followed her gaze, spotting individuals huddled in groups up ahead. Many of them carried long sticks with balls of fire at the top. They all marched on, some even leading small children. As we continued, more individuals emerged, all turning down a street ahead.

I instantly felt on edge. "I'm not sure," I murmured. "But let's be careful." I took my sister's hand with my free hand and pulled her closer to the houses. She snatched her hand back almost instantly. We stuck close to the houses, trailing behind the crowd. Thankfully no one seemed to pay us much mind.

The road led to a small field encircled by trees. Those we followed filled in along the tree line, leaving the center of the field clear. In the center stood a large contraption with a rope tied at the edge. I felt my heart leap as I noticed regulators standing around the contraption. Quickly, I pulled Olivia into the shade of some nearby trees where we could hide. She stayed quiet, her eyes wide as the regulators started to address the mass of people. Their voices were barely audible through the roaring crowd.

I leaned against a tree, peeking around to get a better view. Olivia leaned forward as well, both of us remaining quiet. I could barely see above the crowd. Thankfully, the crowd died down a bit so we could hear a little better.

"I am not ashamed of the Gospel!" A scrawny man in the center, surrounded by regulators, called out. Some in the crowd raised their voices again, a few lifting their fire sticks into the air. I leaned forward as the regulators led the man up some steps of the contraption and toward the rope. "I am not ashamed of Christ!" he yelled out again as one of the regulators tied the rope around his neck.

I felt frozen. With my free hand, I reached my hand into my pocket. I tucked my Bible as deep as it would go then wrapped my fingers around my cross necklace, holding it tight. I kept my hand in my pocket, clutching my cross as I thought about Jesus's own death. I turned away as the man was hanged, dropping my gaze to the ground. *Father, forgive them, for they do not know what they are doing.*

Olivia nudged me. "We need to go." Her voice was low but stern.

I took my hand out of my pocket and looked briefly into the crowd that now cheered as the lifeless body floated from the contraption. They were chanting words I could not distinguish. Realizing the regulators were starting to move through the crowd, I instantly turned and dashed after Olivia. We moved swiftly but not fast enough to raise suspicion. As we turned back on the main road, we broke into a run. We did not look back or stop until we reached the pizzeria.

I quickly ducked inside the dark space after my sister. The place looked just as we had left it but now a lot darker. The only light came from the moonlight that flooded in. We headed toward the kitchen, deciding it would be best to tuck our food away with the rest of the pantry stash. After taking out our new clothes, we stashed our bagged treasure alongside the rest of the food. We placed our clothes on top of the water crates, mine on the bottom right shelf while Olivia briefly organized hers on the left side. We each took a few big gulps from the water gallons we had opened earlier.

"I'm going to sleep on one of the booths." Olivia sounded emotionless. It was obvious we were both in shock from what we just witnessed. I followed my sister out of the pantry then out of the kitchen, making sure to close both doors behind us. I knew we could always talk tomorrow about the day's events. Besides, my sister liked to decompress before any major conversation.

Olivia climbed into one of the bigger booths in the corner, right outside the kitchen door. I chose a booth a bit closer to the entrance, wanting to protect her just in case something were to happen. Although I felt safe here, I was still on edge with this being our first night alone and also from what we had just watched unfold in the city. The world outside these old walls was scary and full of uncertainty, but I somehow felt certain that at least for tonight, we would be safe.

I shifted against the booth, resting on my back with my hands folded behind my head to create a makeshift pillow. It was not nearly as comfy as my bed back at the orphanage, but it would have to do for now.

"Goodnight, Olivia!" I called out.

"Goodnight, Oliver!"

I felt a smile creep across my face as I thought of a way to raise our mood after what we just saw. After a few seconds of silence, I repeated with an accent, "Goodnight, Olivia!"

"Goodnight, Oliver."

I let a few more seconds pass before teasing her again. This time, making my voice high, I squealed, "Goodnight second and thus inferior spawn of my parental units."

"Hey!" Olivia called through the darkness. "I'm pretty sure *I* was born first. But even then, that wouldn't make me inferior!" I heard her sigh. "Now, *goodnight*, Oliver."

"Okay. Goodnight." I figured I'd teased her enough. Yawning, I pulled my legs close to my chest and rolled over. *Ah, much better.* As I closed my eyes and breathed deeply to settle down, I began my nightly prayers. Halfway through my prayers, I pulled out my cross necklace. I felt strength run through me as I traced my fingers along the solid silver cross. I strung it around my neck, tucking it safely underneath my shirt while praying I could embody the same boldness as the martyr from tonight.

Chapter Six

I woke to sunshine blazing through our small restaurant. Everything was still and silent except a few bird chirps outside. While this booth was not nearly as comfortable as my bed back at the orphanage, it wasn't a bad place to rest after a long day. I had slept soundly through the night to my surprise.

As I climbed out of the booth, I glanced over to where Olivia was resting. She was still curled up, her eyes shut tightly. I was careful to not make any noise as I slowly made my way across the restaurant to the restrooms tucked away next to the jukebox.

The two black doors on either side led to identical rooms with white tile floor, dark green walls, a toilet in the left corner, and a sink to the right. I quickly did my business, then re-entered the dining room, crossing it with light steps as Olivia snored away. I ducked behind the kitchen door, wondering what time it was as I grabbed new clothes from the pantry. As I dressed for the day, I thought back to last night's events. Recalling the cries from the martyr, I decided to keep my cross necklace on, tucking my pocket Bible into the pockets of my new basketball shorts.

After folding my dirty clothes and setting them beside the rest of my clothes, I grabbed some cheese to munch on. I was not a big breakfast person but knew I had to get some food in me while I had the chance to do so.

The pantry door creaked open, causing me to pause before taking my first bite. Olivia ambled into the space with a big yawn.

"Well, good morning, sleepyhead!"

"Good morning," she said as she shuffled through her new clothes. "Do you mind staying in here while I change out there?"

"Go for it," I said before stuffing a handful of cheese into my mouth. After a few handfuls, I switched to a deli sandwich while I waited for my sister. When she returned to the pantry, she had on a bright yellow shirt and some tan shorts with black socks tucked into her white sneakers. She placed her old clothes next to her new ones before grabbing some onion rings and a slice of pizza from yesterday's stash.

"It feels amazing to be in new clothes," Olivia said, biting into an onion ring. "Mine from yesterday were getting a little sweaty."

"Oh, trust me." I swallowed a bite of my sandwich. "It was more than a *little* sweaty."

"Well, you're always stinky." Her gaze rested on my cross necklace. "You're not going to wear that out, are you? You saw what happened yesterday." Her voice was stern but full of worry. "The government is *not* a fan of other religions."

"I know, but Christ is worth it." I grabbed hold of my necklace. Although no one had raised us in a religion, I took an interest in it after some adults at the orphanage started gathering in the evening to worship together. The person of Jesus fascinated me and the more I learned about Christian roots and theology, the more I wanted to know. It wasn't long before I began experiencing God's presence comforting me and guiding me. Olivia, on the other hand, remained apathetic to faith as we grew. Nevertheless, she did an excellent job of respecting my beliefs. I knew her concern was not with the cross itself but what would happen if a regulator spotted it.

I tightened my grip on the cross. "Look, I'll put it under my shirt when we go out. That way no one will know." I took another bite out of my sandwich, nearly finished with it.

Olivia nodded. "Okay." She finished her handful of onion rings. "I just don't want to lose you."

I wrapped my arm around her as I finished the remainder of my breakfast. "You won't," I said, hugging her tightly. "I promise." Olivia hugged me back for a few minutes before pulling away. As she did so, I jumped back in surprise as fingers stabbed the sides of my torso simultaneously.

"Ouch!" I glared at my sister as she giggled. "Olivia! Why can't you leave that move back at the orphanage?"

Her eyes narrowed. "With no one else to poke, you'll have to be on your guard *always*." Her words held a playful tone.

I wrapped my arms around myself, securely covering the sides of my torso with my hands. "Just finish up." I motioned toward the slice of pizza she had nearly devoured. "I want to actually do something today."

"Alright, alright!" she chimed, taking a big bite. She glanced around the space as she chewed, peering into the kitchen as well. "If we're going to stay here, don't you think we should decorate a bit? Make it more like a home? It would be nice to move some booths in here. That way we won't have to sleep so out in the open. Plus," she said, running her fingers through her tangled hair, "I'd love to go find a hairbrush somewhere."

"Definitely." My hair was a bit wild, too. "But how are we going to move the booths? They're connected to the walls *and* the floor." I certainly agreed with her, though. Anyone lurking around at night could easily access the pizzeria through the open side. We would be much safer behind the kitchen door.

Olivia strolled toward the kitchen, wiping her hands on her pants after finishing the pizza slice. I followed swiftly. "I'm sure we can find a way to get some of the cushions off," she said, opening a drawer. After rumbling through it for a bit, she pulled out a large knife. I jumped back. I had never seen such a big knife before.

She handed the knife to me, taking out a second one. "If they don't easily come off, we can try cutting them."

I nodded, understanding her plan. Grabbing the handle of the knife, I placed it down at my side as the two of us exited the kitchen into the large dining space. She stopped before the closest booth. Placed her knife on a table, she lifted up the cushion as far as it would go.

"Okay," she said as she reached for the knife. Continuing to hold the cushion up, she gently cut along the bottom of the cushion. "Here's what we're going to do . . ."

***

"You're goin' to draw a turtle?"

"Yeah! It's my favorite animal!"

I am a five-year-old with a single mission: draw the perfect turtle on the blank paper in front of me. Picking up a broken green crayon, I begin to work diligently, sketching and shading in my turtle. While an adult might not see anything other than a green blob, I considered my drawing the finest masterpiece.

The young boy who had questioned me watched intently from across the table. He had paused working on his masterpiece to observe mine. I had known this boy, Caleb, for as long as I could remember. He was also born underground during the height of the war. His jaw stuck out at an angle, which caused his teeth to protrude outside of his mouth. Standing up to the kids who teased him over his looks led to Caleb and me becoming fast friends.

"Fish are my favorite animal," he said, sitting back down in his chair. His paper had a few orange fish drawn on it.

"We know," I muttered back, not even bothering to look up as I added the final touches to my drawing. Caleb was *very* talkative and an open book. He had informed nearly everyone in the bunker of his love for fish. While he chatted with everyone, I found myself a bit more on the quiet side, only wanting to talk to those I knew well.

"Ollie, are you done?"

I lifted my head to find Olivia watching me anxiously. I looked around, finding myself out of my memories about Caleb and back at the pizzeria with my sister. Reality sunk in as I glanced around the kitchen we had attempted to make our own. Some booth cushions were spread out on the floor to make makeshift beds. We had also dragged several dining chairs into the kitchen, one of which I sat on now next to the island counter that had become our dining table. I pushed the leftovers we had gathered from the previous day away from me.

"I'm done." Lunch had been satisfying, much more so than yesterdays, but I was full. "You can have the rest."

Olivia instantly started to pick at the crumbs. "What was going through your mind, if you don't mind sharing? You looked pretty out of it."

"I was thinking about Caleb." I laid my head down on the counter. The memory of us drawing lingered in the back of my mind. We had colored a lot together as kids and played various games outside once we were out of the bunker. Olivia often played outside with us, and the three of us eventually became close.

"Caleb?" Olivia echoed. "I wonder what our old friend is up to."

If he's still alive. The thought made me shiver. It was impossible to know exactly what happened back at the orphanage, but I knew it wouldn't have been good for our dear friend. His looks meant the regulators would instantly classify him as "unworthy," a term I loathed. If my sweet friend was not worthy enough to inherit the new earth the emperor was ordering the regulators to create, then I wanted nothing to do with their "perfect" world.

"I'm sure Caleb is fine." I did not want to imagine otherwise — I couldn't. "Besides," I straightened up. "Maybe he escaped like we did!" I knew it was unlikely, but I did not want to linger in hopelessness.

Olivia wiped her hands on a kitchen towel after finishing what was left of the food. "I hope so!" She crumpled up the bag that had contained our leftovers, then set it down on the counter. "We might need this for later."

I got up, tucking the chair in behind me. "You ready to trek into the city?"

Olivia gave a small smile. "Let's go!"

The two of us ventured out of the kitchen, through the dining space, and into the blazing midday sun.

"Should we try the same alleyway or look somewhere closer for food?" Olivia asked as we emerged into the open.

"In this heat? Let's try to find somewhere closer."

We headed down the street, making sure to walk with the same posture as the city folks. The few trees along the walk offered some shade from the sun's intense rays and bird chirps cut through the stale air. We turned onto a new side street which appeared just as abandoned as ours.

"Oliver, look!" My sister gasped out, pointing to a large house on the edge of the street.

From what I could observe, it looked exactly like every other run-down, abandoned house. It was an old, two-story house with yellow panels and a crumbling front porch. Some of the railing had completely fallen and the front door was loose at the hinges.

"What about it—"

Before I could finish my sentence, Olivia took off toward the house. I chased after her, pondering what might have sparked her interest in the random home. She led me right through the old front door before stopping suddenly. I peeked around her shoulder into a narrow hallway. The wooden floors were covered in dirt and the wallpaper had started piling up at the bottom of the walls. Up ahead appeared to be a small kitchen by the change from hardwood floor to tiles. A closed door stood to the left of us, and stairs were off to the right.

"I am *not* going farther," I spat out, glancing around the dimly lit home. The place was eerie.

"Oh yes you are!" Olivia said, grabbing my arm and tugging me toward the stairs.

"You better have a good reason for dragging us in here!"

"Just hush and come on! You dragged me into an abandoned restaurant, remember? It's my turn now!"

"Yeah, because that looked cool. This is just creepy!"

Olivia rolled her eyes, yanking me closer to the stairs. "Just come on. *Please.*"

I sighed, allowing her to pull me farther into the house. "Okay."

I trailed behind her up the creaky old wooden staircase. The stairs ascended to another hallway, lined with a few closed doors on the left. To the right was an open space with windows overlooking the street we had raced down moments before. The sunlight flooded through, illuminating the empty space. The only piece of furniture was an old wooden wardrobe tucked into the room's corner.

Olivia walked toward the middle window, peering out. I peeked over her shoulder as we stared down at the street below.

"There was . . . I thought I saw . . ."

"Yes?" I moved a hand along the old wall. Paint crumbled under my fingertips as I traced around the window. I shook it off, wiping my hand on my shorts.

Olivia sighed, turning her back to the window. She cast her gaze down. "I could have sworn I saw someone our age standing here."

"Are you sure, Liv? It could have been your mind playing tricks on you." I looked behind us at the closed doors, which now gave off a sinister feeling. There was no telling who or what was hiding behind them.

"I know what I saw!" She shook her head, walking away from the window to the wardrobe. I followed a few steps behind her, my heart starting to race. I breathed out in relief as she opened it to find nothing.

As she closed the doors of the old piece of furniture, a loud bang outside made us both freeze. I raced back to the window, terror gripping my heart as I looked out.

A regulator car was parked on the street below, right in front of the house. I watched in horror as a regulator stepped out, his blond hair slicked back and his jet-black uniform ironed perfectly. I felt my pulse quicken as I noticed another regulator step out with a gun in hand.

Before they had the chance to spot me, I dropped down beside my sister. She was shaking badly.

"We have to hide *now*," I whispered, crawling toward the wardrobe.

"I'm so sorry!" Olivia blurted out. "I shouldn't have brought us here; I just got excited to see another person our age. I thought perhaps they could help us, but it was stupid. This is all my fault!"

I opened the wardrobe and climbed inside. "You didn't know regulators would show up." I reached my hand out, noticing tears glistening in the corners of her eyes. "Quick, I'll help you up!"

She took my hand and instantly climbed up to sit next to me. I closed the doors as tightly as I could, beginning to pray as my thoughts raced. Olivia wrapped her arms around me, burrowing her face into my shoulder. The two of us huddled together, our breath quick. All I could do was hold onto Olivia tightly and pray the regulators would not check our hiding spot. My heart sank as I heard the front door creak open.

The regulators had found us.

Chapter Seven

Olivia shifted beside me as another creak sounded below us. Her breath was hot against my shoulder. I struggled to keep my own breath steady as I breathed in and out deeply through my nose. My eyes focused in the dark, tracing the old wooden pattern of the wardrobe's door that held us securely while regulators climbed the stairs. With every creak I felt my heart quicken until it rung in my ears.

A loud hissing erupted from the hallway just steps away from our hiding spot. I turned to my sister with a confused look. *A cat?* She looked just as perplexed.

One of the regulators shouted inaudible commands as more hisses cut through the silence. The other regulator said something muffled back. Their footsteps continued to creak down the hall.

"Got it!" One of the regulators yelled out between lots of hissing. I heard what sounded like metal clashing for a brief moment before the creaks grew softer as the regulators descended the stairs.

Olivia placed a hand against the door. Before she could open it, I reached my own hand out to stop her. I wanted to be absolutely sure the regulators were gone before making any noise. After a few more moments, I nodded, and she pushed open the wardrobe door.

I instantly crawled to the nearest window to peer out. The regulators were sitting in their car, chatting to each other. In the backseat was a large metal cage. Inside the cage I caught a glimpse of a brown tabby moving around. I assumed the cat was probably still hissing from her open mouth. Olivia peeked out next to me as the car drove away.

She turned away from the window, taking a few steps toward the hallway. "That was so close."

"Too close." *We can't keep getting into these types of situations*, I thought. *Or the regulators will surely catch us.* I got up from the ground and came to her side. "Let's check around for food and supplies then get out of here." Although the regulators were gone, I knew they could come back at any second.

Olivia nodded, approaching the doors across the hall. After trying all of them and realizing they were locked, we quickly descended the stairs to the lower floor. The house was barren apart from a few old pieces of wooden furniture. After searching through the kitchen cabinets, we came across crackers still in their box, a bag of chips, and a half-full container of pretzels.

"Alright, let's get out of here," I said as Olivia swooped the snacks into her arms. Without further hesitation, we dashed down the main hallway toward the front door. As we emerged back out into the hot and humid outdoor air, a small cat jumped onto the porch. It paced toward the front door, licking its lips.

"Another one?" Olivia asked as the silver tabby brushed against her legs before strolling into the house. We watched in amazement as it sprinted up the stairs.

"Huh." I turned my gaze back toward the street, taking a few steps down the crumbling old stairs. "Must be a lot of strays in the area. Perhaps people's pets before the war."

"They look a little too chubby to be strays," Olivia pointed out, coming to my side as we walked through the overgrown yard. "Maybe someone is feeding them."

"Well, I'm not interested in sticking around to find out."

As we continued down the street away from the house, I glanced back one final time. If the cats were looking for their owner or someone to feed them, an empty house surely did not seem like the right place.

***

I kicked out my feet. The ground was hard and cold against my exposed back. Besides an old streetlight a few blocks away, complete darkness surrounded me. Only a couple stars glistened overhead.

As I rolled over and climbed to my feet, I scanned the area. It was an unfamiliar part of town and Olivia was nowhere to be found. As I looked around at the abandoned homes and shops, a car came roaring down the street. I turned to face it, lifting my hands to block out the bright headlights.

I screamed, falling back down as the car zoomed by. The strong wind that blew ruffled my hair.

"Hey, you!"

I peered through the darkness, searching hopelessly for the source of the voice. A figure slowly emerged from the shadows. My heart raced as he came into view, his hair slicked back and his regulator uniform shining in the dark. I sprang up, instantly racing away. I ran with no sense of direction; I just knew I had to get as far away as possible. My feet glided easily over the sidewalk, and I felt as though I were flying.

I cast a quick glance over my shoulder. *NO!* The regulator was keeping pace. As my eyes adjusted even more to the dark, I noticed the regulator reach for his pistol. Gulping, I turned back around and forced myself to go faster. I leaped over holes and cracks in the road, my heart thumping against my chest. Goosebumps spread all over my body as I felt warm breath against the back of my neck.

Trees and houses flashed in the corner of my vision as I gained speed. I pressed onward as the road narrowed. My pulse and breath raced as did my feet. I jumped down the sidewalk, screaming as a gunshot rang through the air.

The regulator yelled out, but I paid him no mind. *I have to keep going.* I raced through the streets, feeling the darkness closing in on me. *Don't look back!* The houses towered over me, some appearing to now have intimidating faces. I peeled my eyes away, keeping my focus straight ahead as I searched desperately for Olivia or our cozy pizzeria. As a hand grabbed the back of my shirt, I let out an ear-piercing scream.

"Oliver, stop!"

I shouted on, kicking my feet each and every way. I kept my eyes closed tight, terrified of whatever was about to happen next.

"Ollie, please!"

I peeled my eyes open. My screaming came to a halt once I realized I was back in the pizzeria on my makeshift bed. I sat up slowly as my eyes adjusted to the dimly lit kitchen that had become our home. Olivia was sitting up in her bed, which bordered mine, her eyes wide as she watched me. Her hand rested against my back in an attempt to calm me. In her other hand was an old mug, one of many we had found in the kitchen's drawers. She offered the cup to me, and I slowly took a few sips of the icy water.

"Bad dream?" Olivia's eyes remained wide as she watched me.

I nodded, placing the cup down.

Olivia pulled her knees toward her chest, wrapping her arms around her legs. "Do you want to talk about it?"

"I was being chased by a regulator," I told her, feeling myself start to calm down. "I was out at night in the city, some neighborhood I didn't know. No matter how fast I ran, he was right behind me. You woke me up just as he grabbed me."

Olivia pulled her legs closer, resting her head on top her knees. "I won't be able to wake you up when it happens in real life. Once they catch us, it's over." Her voice got softer and softer as she spoke. I had to strain my ears to catch the end.

"They won't catch us." I had to stay confident. *I can't linger in despair*, I decided. *That'll just make everything worse.*

"What about yesterday at that old house? We *barely* escaped, Oliver. If they're out here looking for stray cats, then they're lurking in the area. It's only a matter of time until they catch us like they caught that cat."

I stayed quiet, not sure how to respond. She was right. We had gotten lucky yesterday, but it was uncertain if that luck would stay. Each time we trekked into the city there was no guarantee we would make it back home. Every night we returned safely to our pizzeria was a blessing.

"Those cats did seem pretty well fed," I thought out loud, thinking back to yesterday. I glanced up at my sister. "You sure you saw someone in that window?"

She sighed, shrugging her shoulders. "I thought I did, but perhaps I imagined it."

I thought about the locked hallway doors. "I don't think it was your imagination. After all, why would an abandoned house need locked doors?"

Olivia met my gaze, furrowing her eyebrows. "Do you think some-one is hiding out in there, possibly the owner of the cats?"

I glanced into her dark blue eyes; positive she was connecting the dots as well. "The cats did seem friendly and certain of that house."

Olivia smiled, shaking her head and looking downwards. When she met my gaze again, her face was relaxed. "I know what I saw," she said, tilting her head slightly. "But tell me, what does it mean?"

I grinned, knowing she had already figured it out.

"We go back."

Chapter Eight

"We'll check once more, but we can't keep lingering at an empty house."

I led my sister out of the pizzeria in the direction of the old yellow house. We had stopped by frequently in the weeks following our first visit but left each time with no new answers. After spotting another cat entering the old building, Olivia became even more insistent that we go back. After bugging me about it all week, I finally gave in to another visit.

"What if we missed something?" Olivia asked before letting out a big sneeze. She had begun sneezing quite regularly the past couple days and coughed often throughout the night, keeping us both up.

I rolled my eyes. "We've searched the entire house multiple times now. If we don't find anything this time, can you *please* let this whole house thing go?"

"Only if we don't find anything."

As we turned onto the familiar street, we both stopped in our tracks. The houses, except a few, were *gone*. We took it all in as our steps led us closer to the site of the old house which was now reduced to a pile of ash and debris. All that remained were some porch steps now leading to nowhere.

Olivia inched closer to the pile of ash, beginning to inspect the site.

"This is all so strange," I mumbled, glancing at the neighboring house that was also a pile of ash. The house next to it was still standing, just as abandoned and empty as usual. Questions swirled in my mind as Olivia walked around the destroyed homes. *Did a fire break out? If so, why did it only impact some houses and not others?* I could not make sense of the situation. *Why are some homes gone and others still standing?*

"I wonder what happened," Olivia remarked as she returned to my side.

I remained quiet, continuing to look around at the half-burnt street. I looked back at my sister, who was chewing away at her nails. She dropped her hand, raising an eyebrow before speaking again.

"I'm nervous! What about the cat and the person in the window? Someone was here, Ollie. I refuse to believe otherwise!"

I placed my hand on her shoulder, but she instantly shrugged it off. "Whoever it was Liv, they're gone now. We won't find them here."

"I think—"

A loud meow interrupted Olivia. My hope rising, we turned to find the same silver tabby we had seen during our first visit to the house. The cat swished its tail and meowed again before dashing off between what was once two houses. Olivia grabbed my hand as she took off after the cat.

The tiny feline took us deeper into the abandoned neighborhood. We ran past countless streets lined with deserted homes. I couldn't help but wonder what memories the old houses held and how many families had played in the front yards now overgrown with weeds. My heart sank as I realized just how much joy and life this part of the city must have held before the war. The horrors of war had turned a once beautiful neighborhood into a ghost town.

I shook the thoughts away as the cat led us down another street. This time the road ended in a cul-de-sac with houses as hollow as the rest. The sidewalk lining the street crumbled and weeds stuck out here and there. A streetlight laid across the road, glass pieces scattered around it. Amazingly, the green street sign at the end of the street still stood tall. The white letters read *Wallis Court.*

I paused to catch my breath as the cat disappeared into one of the houses. Olivia tugged my arm, taking a few steps forward. "Come on! I saw where the cat went!"

I shook her off. "Forget the cat." I nodded toward the house right of us. "We've got company."

Olivia gasped as a young girl, presumably around our age, stepped out of the shadows. She was small, with golden blond locks, green eyes, and freckles against fair skin. In her ear was what appeared to be a hearing aid and against her hip was an empty bucket. Another girl emerged from the shadows along with two boys, the three of them a dark bronze complexion. The second girl smiled as she glanced us over, her dark hair braided in the front and ending in an afro. Their warm brown eyes narrowed as they looked us over. They gathered around the blond girl, the smaller of the two boys shifting to hide slightly behind the taller boy. Despite their rough state and ragged clothes, all of them were beautiful.

"Who are you, and why are you here?" The blond girl asked as she came to a stop in front of us. From the way she took control, I guessed she was the leader despite one of the boys being taller and looking older. Olivia came to my side, linking her arm with mine as the group towered over us.

"We followed the cat!" Olivia pointed to the house it disappeared into.

For a moment, the blond looked confused. She shook the confusion away and turned to the taller boy. "Chester?"

The boy returned her gaze. "It's your choice."

The girl turned her focus back to us, her green eyes darting from me to Olivia then back again. "Who are you all, and where did you come from?"

I cleared my throat. "My name is Oliver, and this is my twin sister, Olivia. We found shelter in an abandoned building not too far from here. We really mean no trouble and we can get going now. We didn't mean to interrupt anything—"

"Wait!" The girl interrupted me, her gaze softening. "You two are alone out here?" Her gentle and soothing voice instantly made me feel safe.

Olivia and I glanced at each other before we each gave a small nod.

The girl tilted her head slightly. "So, you're not living in the city? You're not with the regulators?"

"Oh, goodness no!" I exclaimed. "We're what they call unworthies."

Olivia tugged my arm, and I realized I was giving away a lot of information. I closed my mouth to stop from saying more.

"Don't call yourself that," Chester said sternly. His tone also had a hint of gentleness to it that instantly made me feel I could trust him. "It only gives others the right to call you that. No one is unworthy."

"That's a good point." The blond turned to meet his gaze. "But if we reclaim it, and call ourselves it first, then when regulators say it, it doesn't hurt as much."

The other girl rolled her eyes. "Y'all, there's two strangers in front of us. Can you all talk about this later, after we decide what to do with them?"

After we decide what to do with them. The girl's words echoed through my mind as four sets of eyes turned to rest on me and my sister. *Who are these people?* I wondered, taking a step back. *Are they like us?*

The blond girl narrowed her eyes for a second before her expression softened again. "Of course," she said with a small smile. "My name is Carlotta. And this is Chester, Kailey, and Trevor." She nodded first at the tall boy, then at the other girl, then at the smaller boy. "We live out here with others considered unworthy. On the outskirts, just out of reach of where regulators patrol."

"Is it wise to give away so much information?" Chester spoke up. From what I was picking up on, it appeared Chester was second in command.

Carlotta turned to meet his gaze. Her posture was much more relaxed now and her voice even more gentle. "They are like us. We can trust them." Chester gave a nod of approval and Carlotta turned back to Olivia and me.

"If you'd like, you can come with us," she offered.

I turned to meet my sister's eyes. She shrugged and nodded.

"Okay," I said softly. I knew it would be good to have friends in the area, and they might have food and supplies.

Carlotta motioned and the group started to head back in the direction they had emerged from. Olivia and I tagged along slowly, her arm still linked in mine.

"Welcome," Carlotta said to us as we exited the cul-de-sac and entered the next abandoned street. "If you were able to trust a cat, you should have no problem trusting your fellow unworthies."

Chapter Nine

"If we continue to attack in numerical order, the regulators might suspect we're coming. I believe switching things up could give them a lovely surprise."

Heads turned to the source of the voice, a petite woman with golden beige skin and jet-black hair that rested just above her shoulders. She sat at the head of the long wooden table, her back straight and her arms relaxed. Placed on the table in front of her was a manila folder and a pink water bottle. She held her head high as her sharp, narrow eyes scanned around to meet the gaze of those gathered. Although she was arguably one of the smallest in the room, her leadership was well respected.

Her assistant, a short, pale fellow with neatly trimmed brown hair, shifted forward slightly in his chair to the left of her. "Agreed." Her dark brown eyes shifted to meet his as he spoke. "But now the question becomes, do we strike station four or five?"

"Well, Dallas, five would be most unpredictable." She turned her eyes back to the rest of those gathered, adjusting her glasses as she did so. "We've already taken out the first two stations, so they'd be expecting us to go for three. Five is also relatively close to their headquarters in Center City, which could give them a scare. How does everyone feel about this?"

A few heads nodded as those gathered began to converse with those around them. While most were seated somewhere around the table, many individuals stood. Word had gotten around town and interest had piqued after the last two successful missions to take out regulator stations. The meeting room in the former fallout shelter was getting a bit tight as more and more individuals showed curiosity in striking back at the government.

"Alright, I think that's enough!" The leader called through the chatter. Heads turned back in her direction as the noise died down. "What have we decided?"

"Ms. Harriet," a girl seated a few chairs down from Dallas spoke up. "Catherine and I believe it would be good to plan the attack for station five. If we go in numerical order, then they will eventually catch on if they haven't already. And like you mentioned, five will give them a scare, that we're here and serious, you know? That we aren't going away. We feel that going for the last station would be the best way to show our strength."

A few heads nodded in agreement. "Yes," a man standing against the wall chimed in. "Max and I agree."

Harriet straightened back up, moving her fingers along the edges of the manila folder. "Then it's decided." She lifted her gaze to look around the room. "We'll go for station five. Report back to your groups, and let them know we'll meet back here at dusk tomorrow. Go now in peace, for this meeting has ended. And remember, we are the Uprising, and the future depends on us."

The room erupted into chatter as the meeting closed. Some individuals left instantly, while others hung around to chat. Harriet picked up her water bottle and the manila folder then proceeded out of the room. Dallas followed as she entered the next room over and flicked on the lights.

The overhead lights slowly buzzed on, revealing a small room. Although guns were few and rare, they had managed to steal some from regulator stations during prior attacks. They had also gathered bows and arrows from hunters, along with hand grenades over the years. The weapons lined the space, and orange and green flags were tucked in a corner. Harriet picked up a bundle of arrows, inspecting each piece briefly before placing them back down.

"Dallas, we need to ensure all this is ready for tomorrow," she called out as her assistant reached her side.

"I already looked through everything before the meeting," he said, his voice steady.

Harriet put down a gun she had been inspecting. "Everything looks good, then." She glanced over to where her assistant now leaned against a small table.

"Always one step ahead." Dallas raised an eyebrow briefly, his gaze soft.

"I really appreciate you; I hope you know that," Harriet said as she came to lean against the table as well. "You may be a bit stubborn at times, but you always get the job done."

Dallas shrugged with a laugh. "I do what I can to fight for those no longer with us."

"I know your brother would be proud of all you've done in his memory."

Dallas dropped his eyes, losing his smile for a brief second. His eyes were a bit watery as he met Harriet's eyes again. "Thank you," he whispered. He got up slowly, picking up a small orange flag tucked into the corner. He pulled it close to his chest as memories of his brother filled him briefly. He had chosen the color as it resembled the orange wristband his brother always wore, a wristband he was still wearing when shot dead by regulators. Dallas sniffled as Harriet came to his side, picking up a green flag. This color had been her choice, a dark forest green that resembled the emeralds her mother wore. Taking a few deep breaths, the two placed the victory flags back in the corner before exiting the room.

"Tomorrow," Harriet broke the silence. "We'll be waving those flags in memory of those we've lost, just think how great it will feel!"

Dallas stayed silent, letting her words sink in and reach his heart. He knew she was right, and her dedication greatly inspired him. All he wanted was to create a better society, one where all people could be accepted and live freely without fear. He straightened up as memories of his brother flashed through his mind. He could only hope that somehow, his brother truly was proud of him.

Chapter Ten

Carlotta and her squad led us deeper into the neighborhood. We passed countless abandoned houses and a few small stores, all of which crumbled away. The majority of houses were boarded-up and a few even had smashed-in windows. Vines crept up the side of buildings and weeds jutted out from the street and sidewalk. As we passed house after house, I couldn't help but imagine how vibrant this place must have once been.

How do they remember all these streets? I wondered as we turned into another run-down neighborhood. Olivia and I had always taken the same route to get to and from the pizzeria. I was grateful to have her by my side; I couldn't imagine doing this on my own. The winding city streets felt like a maze.

I glanced over at Carlotta and her friends. She and Chester led the group while Kailey and Trevor brought up the rear behind Olivia and me. All of them had a relaxed posture and walked with ease unlike those in the city. They seemed so confident walking out in the open despite none of them matching what city folks were to look like. As we marched on, I studied them and wondered what made them unworthy. Other than Carlotta's hearing aid and their refusal to assimilate to societal beauty standards, I couldn't find much. Kailey met my gaze as I glanced her over, causing me to instantly look away. Olivia shifted closer to me as I did so.

"Liv, you okay?" I asked her as she unlinked her arm from mine.

She nodded, her eyes straight on the path ahead. She began to chew her nails as Kailey came to our side.

"So," Kailey began. "Where you all from?"

"Well, we were living with other unworthies before regulators raided our home," I answered. "Since then, we've been on our own."

"We were underground most of our life," Olivia added. "We were born during the war and raised by practically everyone in our bunker. We've only been on the surface six years. The adults wouldn't even let us see the surface until it was safe and warm enough." She snuffled her nose.

Trevor raced to catch up. "So, you'd be around sixteen years old? Did I get that right?" His voice was high-pitched.

"Yeah . . ." I raised an eyebrow. *How did he guess that?* "How old are you?"

"Same!" Kailey replied. "Most of us are sixteen. Well, except Carlotta. She's seventeen. Oh! And Annie and Jennifer are eleven. And . . ."

"And I'm fourteen!" Trevor interrupted.

Kailey rolled her eyes playfully. "Yes, you are." She took on a more serious tone as Olivia snuffled again. "Bad allergies?" Olivia nodded, wiping her nose on her sleeve. "Don't worry, we've got stuff to help with that. A couple of us get them as well. Did you know allergies were common before the war? Max says it's due to the weather and tree pollen, but I don't know about all that. He's always reading conflicting things in his books."

Carlotta cast her gaze back, briefly pausing her conversation with Chester. "Just a little bit farther!" Her smile was so warm and friendly that I couldn't help but smile back.

"Do regulators patrol here often?" I asked, eager to reach our destination.

"Not where we're going." Carlotta leaped effortlessly onto overgrown grass as the road gave way to a grassy field. The end of the road was so torn up that we all ended up having to leap over it or take large steps to avoid the rough terrain.

"Careful," Chester warned, pausing to ensure each of us crossed safely. Eventually we all made it over, continuing to follow Carlotta through the small field. The field emerged into another area lined with abandoned homes. The houses here were very far apart and in the worst condition I'd seen. Many had crumbled away and caved in at points. It looked as though this street had been abandoned long before the rest of the neighborhood, perhaps even before the war.

Carlotta led us down the street, around the circular end, and through the yards of the two homes at the end. As we approached the back of another house, a boy came into view. He watched us with arms folded across his chest. Freckles covered his tan skin and veins stuck out of his muscular arms. Long brown bangs shielded his icy blue eyes that narrowed as he spotted Olivia and me among his friends.

"Relax, Husker," Carlotta told the boy as he raced to meet us. "We invited them."

Husker kept a stern look but stepped aside to reveal the house he had been protecting. The house was tall with upper floors caving in. The first floor was mostly intact, but some walls had caved in here and there. White exterior paint chipped away while dark red bricks held up the remainder of the house and especially the semi-basement that faced us. A stone patio encircled the back door and the ground sloped upwards on both sides, hiding the space from the street above. The patio was empty except a small round fire pit tucked into the corner. Behind it was a small window with blinds shut tightly. The space looked homey and comfortable.

Carlotta turned to Olivia and me. "Welcome to our hideout."

Husker pushed the door open slowly, gesturing for us to head inside. I shuffled in behind the others, surprised when Husker remained outside in the heat. He closed the door securely behind us.

The room we arrived in was large with various flashlights and lanterns illuminating what would otherwise be a dark basement. The area was open despite a wall separating the two rooms ahead of us. To the left of the wall were bunk beds and a red couch near the door we had come through. To the right of the wall was a space with bean bag chairs and cabinets built in around the room. Books and other knickknacks neatly outlined the shelves, along with stacks of neatly folded clothes. To the right of the bean bag room was a closed door, and next to that, spiral stairs ascended to the upper floor. The carpet of the basement was a soft white and the walls were painted a light yellow. The walls showed no damage, and the ceiling was solid with no cracks.

"Kailey, gather those upstairs and please put this away," Carlotta ordered, handing the bucket to her. "The twins and the others should be up there."

Kailey at once bounded up the stairs. As she did so, Trevor entered the door to our right. He gave a small smile and nod before shutting the door behind him. Carlotta nodded back before turning to my sister and me.

"Again," her voice was gentle. "I welcome you both to our home. Most of us sleep down here since not much is left of the upper floors. Just a kitchen and a bathroom, which either of you may use."

"And Elliot's space is up there," Chester chimed in. "Also," he added, nodding in the direction where Trevor had disappeared. "It's important you all give Trevor his space. He's harmless but has been through a lot. His room is his safe place, and we want to make sure everyone respects his boundaries."

My sister and I nodded, still taking it all in. I felt my interest rising as I repeated Carlotta's words in my mind. *Twins!* Somewhere upstairs was another set of twins! Olivia and I had never met other twins before, and I could tell she was just as excited as I was from her expression. Our eyes turned as some noise erupted at the top of the steps. Slowly but surely, a few teens followed Kailey down the stairs. Those of us below stepped back to give them space.

Immediately behind Kailey was a petite yet curvy fair-skinned girl with shoulder-length blond hair and brown eyes. Colorful yarn bracelets covered her arms; I couldn't help but wonder if she made them.

After her came two smaller girls, whom I guessed were the twins due to their strikingly similar appearance. Bright orange hair framed around their round faces. Their green eyes glowed as they glanced over at Olivia and me. One wore glasses. The twins were both extremely pale and whispered to each other as they came down the stairs. The group of girls came to a halt at the bottom of the stairs, their eyes scanning my sister and me.

Carlotta and Chester took a few steps forward, standing a bit off to the side. Kailey joined Carlotta, handing a tissue to Olivia who thanked her quietly.

"This is Oliver and Olivia," Carlotta announced. "Please welcome them as you welcomed one another."

I noticed even more similarities between the twins as they stepped forward. They wore the same short-sleeved hoodie and similar basketball shorts. Both had a gap between their two front teeth as they smiled at us.

"Hello!" The one without glasses spoke up. "I'm Jennifer, and this is my sister, Annie."

Annie smiled briefly, shifting closer to her sister. I guessed she was the shyer of the two.

"It's good to meet you both," I said, hoping I would remember all these new names and faces.

"And I'm Sidney, but feel free to call me Sid." The other girl said nonchalantly before heading toward the bean bag chairs. The twins followed her, giggling as they looked back at us. The three girls plopped down on a bean bag, still watching us.

My eyes snapped back to the stairs as they creaked. A boy slowly approached us. He had a fair complexion and long, curly brown hair that stopped at his shoulders. His deep brown eyes darted from me to Olivia then back again. He had the brightest smile I'd ever seen, and his eyes had a sparkle to them. I felt instantly drawn to him.

"Apologies for the delay. I've nearly got the laptop up and running!" His voice was just slightly deep. His eyes glanced us over. "It's nice to have some newbies around! I'm Elliot."

I realized he hadn't been present to hear our names. "I'm Oliver, and this is my sister, Olivia."

"Good to meet you both."

Carlotta stepped forward as Elliot dashed back up the stairs. As he left, I noticed he only wore one sock. *Perhaps he lost the other one . . .*

"Our other comrade is out at the moment," Carlotta's voice interrupted my thoughts. "But he should return soon. You're both welcome to stay for as long as you'd like. Please make yourselves at home."

"Thank you so much!" Olivia said, heading toward the bean bags. She took a spot next to Sid. Kailey followed, as did Chester. Carlotta smiled at me once more before heading up the stairs. I watched as she went, glancing back at the group before bounding up after her to find out what was left of the upstairs.

Chapter Eleven

It was dark and quiet as I stepped off the last step and entered the first floor of the house. I stood in a large, open hallway lined with framed pictures of meadows and fruit. The old red wallpaper crumbled around the edges and the carpet was a rough, dirty white. About halfway down the hallway was an open door and beyond that appeared to be a kitchen.

As I passed the open door, I caught sight of a large tub against one wall. Against the other wall was a toilet and sink. It was a dark room with only a singular lantern. *I'll have to bring a flashlight or another lantern with me when I need to go*, I thought.

A quiet giggle caused me to look over my shoulder. Jennifer emerged from the darkness, Annie right behind her.

"Let's scare Elliot and Carlotta!" Jennifer whispered as Annie let out a few chuckles.

"Let's do what?"

Annie held a finger to her mouth. "Shush! Or they'll hear us coming!"

The two girls rushed past me, emerging into the kitchen. Compared to the dark hallway, the kitchen was much livelier with sunlight flooding in from multiple windows. The space was homey with wooden cabinets, a large dining table covered with a blue and white checkered tablecloth, and pink walls. Next to a sink were cups with names scribbled on them.

As I followed the twins through the space, I noticed what appeared to have been another room off to the right. It was now nothing but rubble with multiple blankets covering the top to shelter the space from the outside air. If there was ever more to the house, it was now gone, hidden behind rubble.

"Over here!" Jennifer said softly, giving my shirt a few tugs. I followed her and Annie to an opening in the wall tucked into the kitchen's left corner. Some voices came from behind the wall.

The two girls huddled next to the entrance, giggling quietly as they whispered back and forth.

I crouched behind them, peering around the opening.

After a few more seconds, Annie and Jennifer rushed into the space with loud squeals that quickly turned into laughter. I slowly entered after them.

The room was surprisingly large with old wooden furniture lining the dark blue walls. Blankets and pillows were scattered on top the rugged off-white carpet, and in the middle of the room was a small circular table with an old piece of technology on it. Elliot and Carlotta were on either side of the table, their faces stretched into smiles as they held on to the twins.

"You dare attack Elliot's fortress!" Elliot teased as Jennifer wiggled in his arms, attempting to pull him to the ground. His eyes met mine. "And you brought back up!"

Carlotta giggled as she and Annie crashed to the ground. "Elliot, avenge me!" Carlotta said, pretending to play dead. Annie rushed to help Jennifer.

"Looks like you've been defeated," I snickered as the twins and Elliot fell to the floor. I leaned against an old wooden dresser just feet away. It was bare except for some dust.

"We win!" Jennifer announced, throwing her and Annie's fists into the air. She ran over to me, throwing mine into the air as well. I played along, unable to resist a smile. As she released my hand, Carlotta and Elliot climbed to their feet, smiles lighting up their faces.

"Now I'm hungry," Jennifer mumbled, crossing the room back to the entrance. Annie trailed right behind her, the two eventually ducking out of the space into the kitchen. I watched fondly as they left, then turned my attention to Carlotta and Elliot who nodded to acknowledge my presence.

"They're a lovely pair, aren't they?" Elliot beamed. I noticed he still only had on one sock. "Welcome to my room."

"It's very nice!" I replied, shifting my gaze from his bare foot to my surroundings. "But how did you manage to get a room all to yourself?" I could understand Trevor needing his own space with how skittish and timid the boy was, but Elliot did not give off the same impression. He seemed well adjusted to the world.

He chuckled. "I apparently make too much noise at night."

"He tosses around, which makes too much noise since he refused anything but a top bunk," Carlotta added. "And he kicks and he snores *loudly*." She nudged the boy playfully. "I can't believe we put up with him for as long as we did."

"You've been here a long time?" I asked, coming to their side. My gaze focused on the piece of technology, which was a dark gray device. The alphabet and some buttons lined the bottom half, and a blue screen lit up the top half. I was instantly intrigued. Technology was rare as much of it was destroyed in the war and signals were hard to come across. I had never seen a device that lit up like this one. "What is this thing?"

"Been here about a year now," Elliot answered as he held down one of the buttons. "And it's a laptop. Got it working only a couple minutes ago, but unfortunately there's not much it can do without a signal." He traced his finger along a square piece on the bottom before clicking it twice. Nothing changed.

"Where did you find it?" I asked, my eyes still glued to the device.

"At the old library. Max nearly stepped on it." He broke off with a laugh. "Too bad he didn't step on a charger while he was at it."

"You didn't find chargers while you were out?" Carlotta inquired.

Elliot shook his head. "Nah." With a click of a button, he powered down the device. "I wish though."

Before any of us could speak again, Chester poked his head into the room.

"Max is back," he said, his eyes meeting each of ours. "And he's got exciting news."

Carlotta immediately strode out of the room, chatting with her second in command as she reached his side. Elliot and I glanced at each other briefly before leaving his space. I wasn't sure what was about to happen, but I was ecstatic to meet another member of the group.

Chapter Twelve

The basement was full of chatter as the group crowded around a short, pale boy. Dark brown wavy hair poked out under the edges of his navy beanie. He lifted off a large pair of sunglasses revealing dark brown eyes that glanced around the group. In his right arm he clutched a book to his chest. It appeared all the group had assembled to hear the boy's news. Even Husker stood right inside the door and Trevor leaned against his door.

I pushed through the group, heading for my sister who stood off to the side right behind Sid. "What's going on?" I whispered, reaching her side.

"Max just got back from a meeting with the Uprising."

"The what?" A few adults at the orphanage had mentioned the Uprising, but no one had ever offered an explanation.

Sid turned around. "It's those who resist the government and actively fight back. We've been joining their attacks."

I shifted my focus back to Max as I caught on to what was happening. "They're planning to attack station five. I'll be leaving here slightly before dusk, for anyone who plans to join." His voice was a bit hoarse, and I guessed he also struggled with allergies.

"I'm in!" Kailey stepped forward.

"Me as well." Sid spoke up.

I glanced over at my sister as Carlotta and Elliot also voiced their decision to go. It seemed dangerous but also like a thrilling opportunity. I knew I would be pleased to fight back, especially as I thought of the orphanage. But I wasn't sure how Olivia felt.

"I'll stay behind to guard." Husker's choice surprised me. His muscular arms seemed perfect for a fight. If I had his body, I wouldn't hesitate to get in some good trouble.

"There's an organized resistance?" My question came out louder than intended. The group paused the discussion as eyes turned toward me. I knew people opposed the government but I hadn't realized an organized resistance had taken root.

Max glanced nervously at my sister and me before turning back to Carlotta. "More newbies?"

Carlotta nodded. "Max, this is Olivia and Oliver, a pair of twins we came across."

Max just nodded slightly, still glancing us over. "They look just like city folks! Are you sure we can trust them?"

His words stung, but I knew they held some truth. Olivia and I had the blond hair and blue eyes of the city folks and had even started walking like them out of habit. It made total sense for him to be suspicious of us.

"Yes," Carlotta's voice was stern. "Like I said, they're *twins*. You know the government wouldn't have allowed both to live with their one child policy."

"Right," Max smiled bleakly before casting his gaze away. "Those cowards claim to be all mighty and powerful yet fear a big family challenging them. Anyways," he paused for a second, his lip curling into a smirk as he glanced back at Olivia and me. "Maybe they can prove their twinness by joining us tomorrow."

I clenched my fists, taking a step toward the boy. "You really think we'd lie about that?" I felt a lump in my throat as my chest tightened. "We lost everything because of regulators!" I closed my mouth as Olivia tugged me back. She didn't have to say anything, but I knew. The last thing we needed was a fight. We were greatly outnumbered.

"Yeah? So have the rest of us," Max mumbled.

"Enough!" Carlotta came to stand between us so I could no longer see Max. "This type of behavior is not appropriate, and we will not tolerate it. Max, you welcomed Annie and Jennifer as twins. Welcome Oliver and Olivia as well. They were in the same position you were when I first found you."

Max cast his gaze down. "Fine." He glanced back up to look over the rest of the group. "Anyone planning to join me tomorrow, meet at the back door before dusk. We will leave promptly." Without another word, he headed to one of the bean bag chairs. After settling down, he propped open his book, not looking up once. I unclenched my fists, exhaling as I shook my head. *Everyone's just on edge with the state of the world,* I reminded myself. *It's likely not a personal attack. At least, it better not be!*

The group slowly dispersed with some heading upstairs or to the bean bag chairs. Carlotta quickly came over to Olivia and me as we remained in our spots. Chester followed closely.

"I'm so sorry! I promise he's usually not like that." She glanced briefly at Max who was now buried in his book.

I shook my head, feeling my body start to relax. "No, it's okay, it's to be expected. Really, we don't look like twins. At least not in the way Annie and Jennifer do." The twins were next to Max, one on either side of him as if reading along.

"He'll come around." Chester placed his hand on my shoulder.

"If you two don't want to go, you really don't have to. It's danger-ous and plenty of the group stays back," Carlotta said.

Husker took a few steps away from the back door. "Besides, it's just as important to protect homebase." His gaze was less hard than before.

I glanced at Olivia who returned my gaze. "We'll think it over."

Carlotta nodded, she and Chester eventually joining Husker at the back door to give us some privacy. My sister turned to meet my gaze as we were left alone in the center of the basement.

"What are you thinking?" she asked.

I remained quiet for a bit. I was eager to prove myself to the group but did not want Max's words to appear to be my only influence. I knew deep down I was doing this for myself, and for my sister, and Caleb, and all the others we had to leave behind at the orphanage. The outing would be scary, but I had plenty to fight for.

"I'm going to go," I said, quickly adding, "but you don't have to."

Olivia smiled slightly, raising an eyebrow. "You think I'd pass up the chance to beat some regulator a-double-s?" She rolled her eyes playfully. "I'm coming too."

"Then it's decided." The two of us headed toward Carlotta and the others, who glanced up as we approached them.

"Well?" Carlotta inquired as we joined them. "You all in?"

"I am!" Olivia took a step forward.

After a few moments, I stepped forward myself. "You bet."

Chapter Thirteen

"Let's go this way! I spot some stores up ahead," Olivia called out as we emerged onto a new street. We had decided to venture out after spending the night with the group and indulging in a big breakfast of eggs and fresh fruit with them, the biggest breakfast we'd had in a while. The group had welcomed us as their own and we longed to return with plenty of food as a way to thank them for their generous hospitality. Even Max had shown some interest in us, but I could tell his guard was still up. I knew I shouldn't blame him in these uncertain and desperate times, but I still felt taken aback by his behavior.

I bounded after my sister down the well-maintained street of colorful homes. "We can check behind whatever stores you'd like," I said, lifting up a hand to shelter my eyes from the blazing afternoon sun. As I dropped my hand, it slid across my cross. Remembering my promise to my sister, I swiftly tucked the cross under my shirt. Although I wanted to proudly display it, I did not want to get us in any kind of trouble. At least not until the Uprising attack tonight.

"These flowers are so pretty!" Olivia said, stopping to sniff a rose bush at the edge of a driveway. She plucked one as I leaned down to smell for myself. They gave off a sweet, pleasant scent.

After tracing the flower's petals with her fingers, Olivia tucked the flower behind her braided hair aligned with colorful barrettes. She,

Sid, and Kailey had styled each other's hair before we set out for the day. Olivia turned to me with a smile as I straightened back up.

"Would you like a flower for your hair?" she joked, reaching out her hand and ruffling my hair.

"Stop!" I shook her off and pulled my head back. "You're messing up my hair!"

My sister giggled as she reached for another flower. "Your hair is certainly long enough to hold one!"

"Not that long," I grumbled.

Before she could pick a flower to torture me with, a loud siren sounded. Its screech ripped through the air. I froze as I noticed a regulator car coming down the street.

Olivia yanked the flower out of her hair and shoved it back in the bush. She grabbed my shirt, tugging me as the car came closer. "Oliver, let's go! We've got to run!"

I recalled Max's words about how we looked like city folks. "Don't run," I urged my sister. "That'll cause a scene. Just walk slowly and calmly, in the same way the city folks do. We aren't doing anything wrong."

Olivia looked at me with wide eyes but quickly did as I said, both of us straightening our backs and swinging our arms slightly to mimic the city folks. I focused my gaze ahead as my pulse raced in my ears. I made sure to put one foot perfectly in front of the other, aligning my movements with those in the city. *Please Lord, let my plan work!*

I breathed out a sigh of relief as the car sped past us. *Yes!* My plan had worked. The regulators hadn't suspected us of anything but instead took us to be regular pedestrians. *Maybe Max has a point,* I thought to myself. *Perhaps there's some goodness underneath all that attitude.*

Olivia looked over at me with amazement as the car drove into the distance. Her eyes were still wide. "What, how did, what just . . ." She tilted her head.

"Liv," I said, making sure to continue walking the same way as the city folks even though the car was now out of sight. "Remember what Max said? We have blond hair and blue eyes; we blend right in! Why do you think we've been able to go unnoticed during our treks into the city?" I thought about Max's beanie and sunglasses and how he only removed them once back in the basement. "The others have to hide behind hats and sunglasses when they're in the city!"

Olivia opened her mouth as if to respond then closed it. I could tell from her expressions that she was beginning to connect the dots. She straightened up even more, smiling as we marched onward. *I feel untouchable!* I thought. *The regulators got nothin' on us!*

The two of us continued, eventually arriving at the shops Olivia had pointed out earlier. Among them were some small restaurants. As soon as the coast was clear, we ducked into the alleyway. The space was dark with multiple large trash cans. Olivia ran to the nearest, instantly flipping open the lid. We peered into the trash but found nothing good among the rubbish.

"Let's keep looking," I sighed before heading toward the next one. Wrinkling my nose, I slid the lid off gently and called my sister over.

Olivia raced to my side as I reached in to pull out a half-crumpled bag with a logo on it. Opening it slowly, we found some burgers wrapped in foil. A few were still warm.

"This will be perfect to take back," I said, feeling satisfied with my find.

The two of us continued probing through the waste, eventually finding another bag of wrapped chicken pieces near the bottom. After a thorough search of the can, we moved to the next one. I clutched the bag of burgers tightly while Olivia carried the bag of tenders.

The next trash can didn't contain much. We found a handful of bagels, but the rest of the food was moldy. As I prepared myself to reach back in for a final search, a loud siren screeched from down the alley. Olivia jumped before dashing deeper into the alley. I took off after her, not even caring that neither of us had placed the lid back on the trash can.

Regulators! I felt my breath quicken along with my steps as I sprinted after Olivia. *They can't know we were digging through the trash!* Scavenging for food would be a dead giveaway we were not city folks.

The alleyway emerged into a crowded street lined with regulator cars, a few of them ablaze. People fled the area while others wrestled with regulators. Store windows had been smashed, and glass littered the neatly paved road. The street was in a state of chaos.

I turned to run back down the alley just as three large regulators appeared out of the shadows. Each had perfectly slicked back hair and not a wrinkle was present on their uniforms. I felt Olivia take hold of my hand and slowly pull backwards. I gulped as I glanced around. The road was blocked with cars and regulators. We were trapped.

I tightened my grip on Olivia's hand only to be ripped away as a regulator shoved me to the ground. Pain ran through my body as the regulator slammed me against the hard, hot pavement. He twisted my hands behind my back, locking them in place with a cold device. No matter how much I struggled, I was stuck. I looked up to see two regulators handling Olivia, handcuffing her as well.

"Get off her!" I yelled. I shifted along the hot pavement in an attempt to get closer.

The regulator shoved me back down, tightening his grip on me. He pressed my face into the black asphalt. "Thefts! How dare you steal out of the trash like that!" His harsh tone pierced my ears. "Identify yourselves!"

"Oliver!" I moved my head so that only one cheek rested against the road. Fear consumed my racing heart as I realized I could no longer see my sister, but her scream not far off told me she was close.

"Where are your parents?" The regulator continued to interrogate me, his hot breath rancid. "Why were you desperate enough to feed from another's rubbish?"

I ignored him, my eyes glancing around nervously to locate my sister. I struggled against the regulator and the hard ground, my breath heavy.

"What . . ." I felt the regulator's fingers against my neck. My heart sank as he tugged my necklace, yanking it over my head and glancing at it with a disgusted look. "Are you a Christian? You dare to deny our mighty emperor and claim another as Lord?"

"Jesus is Lord!" I hollered without hesitation as the regulator pulled me off the ground. His large hands rested over my chained ones, causing mine to sweat profusely. He pushed me forward and I felt my heart leap as I noticed Olivia standing against a car, a regulator holding on to her arm and another a few feet off. I was relieved that I couldn't see a single mark or bruise on her. I opened my mouth to cry out but only swallowed air. The world felt like it was spinning.

The regulator brought me to a halt a few feet away from my sister. She raised her teary eyes steadily to meet mine. I wanted nothing more than to hug her close, but the regulator kept a firm grip on me.

"Take them to station three," he instructed the others.

No! That wasn't the station the Uprising was attacking tonight. How in the world were we going to get out of our situation? I sighed in defeat as I realized no one was planning to rescue us.

The regulator holding on to Olivia nodded as another opened the car door to the backseat.

"Don't hurt her!" I wailed as they shoved Olivia into the backseat. The regulator pushed me into the car, slamming the door as soon as I swung my legs in. I shifted closer to my sister while one of the regulators entered the front seat and started the engine.

The car was all black on the inside from the seats to the ceiling. The air that blew through the vents was warm and stuffy, and some noises came through the radio to the right of the regulator's wheel. He pressed a few buttons on the radio's screen before taking off. A netted window separated the front half of the car from the back half.

"You're lucky my hands are tied and this . . . this net is separating us!" I spat out, feeling my cheeks flush and my stomach tighten. I wanted nothing more than to fight the regulator.

"Not another word from you two!" The regulator grumbled, dialing up the radio to drown us out.

I took a few deep breaths, then turned to my sister, who hung her head. She glanced briefly at me, tears rolling down her cheeks. "They didn't hurt you, did they?" Although she appeared physically okay, I could sense how broken she felt.

She turned to meet my gaze more strongly, managing a small smile. "I'm okay."

I kept my eyes locked on her as the regulator sped up. "We're going to make it through this, Liv. I won't let them hurt us. I promise."

She gave me another small smile, resting her head on my shoulder. I felt an urge to reach out to her but alas my hands were tied, so I instead rested my head on hers. I glanced out the window as we drove past trees and city buildings. Having my sister by my side eased my worry slightly and I felt my breath start to stabilize as I relaxed against her.

Please Lord, I silently prayed. *Let us be okay!*

Chapter Fourteen

The regulator drove us deep into the city to a large white building surrounded by metal fences. The inside was just as white with large white halls and fluorescent lights that produced a slight humming noise. The air was stale and the water they gave us in white Styrofoam cups tasted just as stale. The place was dull, boring, and absent of color. I hated it instantly.

Regulators led us down the large main hallway to a smaller one with cells divided by cold metal bars. Each cell had a mattress or two, which took up nearly the entire concrete floor. The room they shoved me into contained a stained mattress and a gray toilet and sink tucked in the corner. The place was cramped.

Olivia was flung into a similar cell next to mine with another girl who appeared to be around our age. The girl glanced up with sad eyes as Olivia was locked up with her. Her hair was dark brown and slightly curly. Her skin and eyes were a similar shade of brown. I reached my arm through the metal bars that separated our cells as Olivia exchanged a few words with the girl. My sister kept making small steps in my direction, her eyes darting between me and the girl.

The metal bar was hard and cold against my skin. *How many others have stood in this exact spot?* I wondered. *What happened to them? What did the regulators do to them?*

I inhaled a shaky breath as I glanced around. A breakout didn't seem possible. The bars were securely in place and the doors holding us had been locked with a key. I attempted to steady my breath as I pondered the fate of those who had been locked up before me, feeling at least somewhat grateful for the cool air that blew in through large overhead vents.

"Liv!" I called out, reaching my hand farther through the bars toward my sister. She moved quickly to my side, wrapping her fingers around my dangling hand as she crouched down beside me.

"I have no idea how to get us out of here," she said, tears forming in her eyes. "Nevaeh was telling me she's been in here for a week." She nodded her head in the direction of the other girl who watched us with wide eyes. "She's tried everything but no luck."

Nevaeh! I thought. *What a pretty name!*

I sighed, taking back my hand to wipe some sweat that had crept on to my forehead. Images of the man we saw hanged flashed through my mind. The regulator that had captured me took my cross, and shortly upon arrival, both of us had been searched, which led to my pocket Bible being confiscated as well. *They know I believe in Jesus.* The thought made my heart sink and chest tighten. I smiled sheepishly at my sister, who had started to bite away at her nails.

"They know I'm a Christian. I doubt they're going to let me live much longer." My voice shook as I held back tears.

Olivia squeezed her eyes shut, dropping her hand away from her mouth as she cast her gaze downward. "No . . ." Her voice was barely audible. "We've got to find a way!"

She traced the metal bars, pulling on them in the hope of any coming loose. None of them gave way. Olivia plopped down to the floor in tears.

I instantly came to a crouch near her, reaching my hands through the bars to grab hold of her. "I'll fight back if I have to," I promised her. It took everything in me to hold back my own tears. Although I wanted to comfort my sister and reassure her everything was going to be okay, I couldn't. Our cells were secure and locked with no way out. Escape was not only unlikely, it seemed impossible. It appeared that our fate at the hands of the regulators was sealed. At least, mine was.

I pulled my hands back into my own cell as I sat all the way down. I folded my knees close to my chest, wrapping my arms tightly around myself in a self-hug. I cast my gaze down as I felt a tear drop down my left cheek. I had never really thought about how I would die. I had never expected to die so young, and I couldn't imagine the pain my sister would have to navigate in my absence. *If only we had gone down another alley! If only we had turned down a different street!* My vision blurred as the tears I'd been holding back poured out my eyes. I turned so my sister and her cellmate wouldn't see me crying. *Am I going to feel a lot of pain or will it be an instant death? Are they going to hang me as well?*

I shook the thoughts away, turning to crawl toward the old, stained mattress. Maybe I could sleep through my death. Maybe they would just come in and shoot me while I rested. Maybe I could fight off the anxiety about my approaching death if I slept it all away. At least that way I wouldn't have to see Olivia's frightened tear-stained face as they killed me.

The mattress was hard with some damp areas. My tears formed another wet spot as I laid my head down slowly. *Oh Lord,* I prayed silently. *I know I've made a lot of mistakes. I know I've sinned against you in thought, word, and deed. But Lord, I thank you for not holding my sins and my past against me and for the forgiveness of sins offered through Christ Jesus. Lord, please have mercy on me as my time approaches. And if you are able and willing, please deliver me, my Lord!*

I sat up as I brought the prayer to a close, taking a deep breath. Everything felt so still and silent except for a buzzing noise coming from the overhead vents. I glanced over at Olivia who was sitting beside Nevaeh on their mattress. Both of their eyes were wide. They whispered back and forth.

What caused her to be locked up? I wondered, glancing over Nevaeh. *And why has she been in here so long?* The longer I looked in her direction, the more I noticed her unique features. Her long eyelashes highlighted her gorgeous chestnut eyes. Her fingernails were painted a pastel yellow and a small blue hairclip was tucked behind her ear. She was stunningly beautiful with a soft and friendly aura.

My admiration of my sister's cellmate was cut short as loud noises emerged from down the hall. I instantly sprung up, the girls doing the same. The shouting got louder as a few individuals raced past us.

"Help! Please help us!" I yelled once I realized those racing by were not regulators. A few more ran by, their dark hair flowing behind them. I tightened my grip on the metal bars, hollering for help as an alarm echoed around us.

"Me next, me next!" I cried as one of the individuals unlocked the cell holding Nevaeh and my sister. Nevaeh sped off while Olivia came to my side, grabbing my shirt through the bars.

"Please!" She begged. "Please, he's my brother, my twin! They'll kill him!"

The individual paused briefly before racing toward my cell. The keys jingled as he frantically tried to open my cell.

"Are you part of the Uprising?" I asked as he turned a key back and forth.

He smiled. "I wish! But nah. Me and some others just broke out of the room they had us in. Even stole their keys." The man looked pleased with himself.

Olivia released her hold on me as the door creaked open and I burst out. "Come on!" The man said as he raced off in the direction of the others. "This way!"

My sister and I took off at once behind the man down another large hallway. We barged through a large metal door at the end of the hall, catching up with some of the others. The man vanished among them. Alarms rang overhead as we sprinted down the halls, searching desperately for an exit.

"This way!" A voice called out through the chaos. Turning in the direction of the voice, I saw an open door that led to the bright outside world. Those ahead of us had started piling through it. I grabbed my sister's hand as we got closer and emerged out into a grassy field.

Up ahead, people climbed the metal pair of fences. Behind them was a fast-flowing river with rocks breaking through the surface. Beyond the river stood woods. *We can do this*, I thought as I drew in a deep breath. *We're almost there.*

I tightened my grip on Olivia's hand as we followed the crowd and started to climb the fence. Only one word escaped my lips as we slipped down to the other side.

"RUN!"

Chapter Fifteen

The two of us continued after the crowd as many of them plummeted into the river. I crouched down, peering into the rushing waters. *Okay,* I drew in a deep breath. *Just one small jump and a quick swim and we'll be safely on the other side.* My head spun as I recalled the swimming lessons we took as kids in the orphanage's bunker. That small, plastic pool was minuscule compared to the roaring current that rushed below us now. I knew this short swim would not be nearly as easy, but I felt certain we could handle it.

I glanced up as Olivia dropped down beside me, swinging her legs over the short edge. "Together," she said with a small nod.

I swung my feet over as well, bracing myself as I watched others struggle against the current. Many had already made it to the other side, quickly disappearing into the woods. *Soon that'll be us!* I felt a rush of excitement knowing my sister and I would soon be safe and heading back into the city away from the regulators. We had been through so much together and had overcome so much. Despite the odds stacked against us, we had made it on our own. I was ready for our next adventure and to be free once again.

"Okay," I said so softly I wasn't sure if I had even spoken at all. Olivia pushed off the edge into the waters below. After one final glance back to see some regulators nearing the fence, I pushed off the ledge as well.

Freezing water swirled around me as I broke the surface, pulling me downstream like a ragdoll. With all my might, I kicked and swung my arms in an attempt to reach the surface. *This is nothing like our swim lessons!* I gasped as my head reached the surface, peeling my eyes open through the sting. I kicked furiously as my vision narrowed, doing my best to keep my head above water.

The stream was vicious but I fought on, eventually starting to close in on the other side. I noticed Olivia a bit behind me, making progress as well. Screams and yells sounded overhead. I couldn't tell if they were from the other escapees or the regulators, but I couldn't care. All I knew was that I had to reach the other side and get out of this water.

Almost there!

I moved my arms frantically, now about an arm's length away from the other side. I stretched my hands out and grabbed onto long grass. Sand stuck to my arms as I pulled myself out of the water and collapsed on the riverbank. I rested my cheek against the grass, which was much softer than the hard mattress and the hot pavement from earlier. *We did it*, I thought as I took some deep breaths. *We're safe.*

I sat up almost as quickly as the thoughts drifted across my aching brain. My pulse quickened once I realized Olivia was not by my side. I crawled back to the water's edge, scanning over the crowd.

"Olivia!" I cried out. A few others climbed out of the water, glancing at me before racing off into the woods. "Liv!" *Where are you?*

There!

To my surprise, she was only at the halfway point. She fought desperately against the current, which pushed her against one of the rocks.

I climbed to my feet, bracing myself to re-enter the cold water. Before I could jump back in, a loud, ear-splitting bang rang through the air. Two more followed it, causing me to freeze and my ears to ring. My racing thoughts came to a halt. I opened my mouth, but nothing came out. As some of the grass and sand exploded next to me, my knees gave out. I crashed back down on the ground, my eyes wide and glued to where my sister was. More and more people crawled out of the water, all with wide mouths and wide eyes. I knew logically they were screaming but all I could hear was a buzzing sound in my ears. I couldn't even hear my own cries.

I forced myself forward, feeling like my tense body wasn't even my own. Every move took tremendous effort. I paused as I placed my hand back into the water that was beginning to show red streaks. To my right an individual was pulled out the water by two others. Blood dripped down his legs as his white shirt began to turn red. His eyes were squeezed shut and his mouth gasped for air.

I slowly looked away, turning my attention back to my sister. Water splashed as bullets cut through the surface. I tightened my grip on the grassy sand below. I felt a hand tug my shirt, pulling me away from the water. I turned slowly to see some of the others shouting at me, urging me to leave the scene. I did my best to shake them off, but it was no use. I was pulled deeper and deeper into the woods as the shots continued.

"No!" My wail ripped through the buzzing. I collapsed among the vegetation as the hands let go. I exchanged one final look with the escapees before they disappeared into the woods, leaving me alone. I peered through some weeds at the now blood-soaked river. A handful of bodies were scattered, pressed up against the rocks or clinging to the riverbank as their legs flowed in the current. The regulators glanced over the scene, talking among themselves before heading back toward the building.

Slowly but surely, the buzzing of bugs replaced the buzzing in my ears. A warm breeze rustled through the trees, drying me off slightly. My clothes clung to my small frame. They felt so heavy, but not nearly as heavy as the rest of me. As soon as the regulators were out of sight, I forced myself up and stumbled to the river's edge.

I sat down at the river's side, my eyes locked on the lifeless body that once held my wombmate, my sister, my twin, my best friend. She was motionless, her arms clinging to the rock. Her eyes were peeled open, her blond hair now had hints of red in it, and her soaked shirt was stained with the same bright red. I drew in a shaky breath as I took in the sight.

I slowly climbed to my feet and re-entered the water. The water's cold sting was nothing compared to the sting of my broken heart.

Chapter Sixteen

I wrapped the intersection of the makeshift cross with some weed stems I'd plucked from the woods. The twigs wobbled a bit as I forced them together but eventually came to rest perfectly in the shape of a cross as I tied them together. I shoved the cross into the sand on top of the last mound.

I stood back, glancing over the area where I'd buried the bodies. I had originally intended to only bury my sister but after realizing no one was coming back for the others, I gently scooped out a grave for each of them in the riverbank's sand. Now, each had their own grave and had received a proper burial. It took hours and I completely lost track of time, but I wouldn't have had it any other way.

A breeze wrapped around me as I slowly made my way back to Olivia's grave in the middle. Each step took tremendous effort. I placed my hand into my pocket, wrapping my fingers around the barrettes she'd been wearing. I clutched them tightly, knowing eventually I'd have to return them to their rightful owner.

Stooping down, I gently scattered the flowers over my sister's grave to be farther apart. The surrounding woods surprisingly contained lots of flowers, and I had picked a generous amount for Olivia.

I remained over the ground that contained her body. My clothes had dried but my body still felt so heavy. *This can't be my reality*, I thought, my eyes burning from crying. I pinched myself, hoping I would awake from a bad dream. *Please Lord, tell me this isn't real! Let me wake up soon, let Olivia shake me awake!*

Standing up, I let out a deep, shaky exhale as the river roared on. The blood was now all washed away despite some stains on the rocks and sand. I gulped, remembering how it had looked just hours prior. One of the rocks was marked with bullet holes.

I raised my gaze to the regulator station, which shone bright against the darkening sky. The bright, artificial lights seemed so out of place among the grassy horizon and the woods that bordered the property. I shook my head, pulling my gaze away from the building and toward my sister's grave.

"Lord," I closed my eyes. "Thank you. Thank you for everything Olivia was. Thank you for her kindness, her bravery, her friendship. For the patience she had with me through the years and the memories we shared. For the way she always had my back, even when we got on each other's last nerve. For the way she always listened." I paused briefly. "Thank you, Lord, for giving me so many years with her. Lord, have mercy on her and everyone else who passed here today. They did the best they could with the short amount of time they had. May they come to rest in your love and in your peace. Amen."

I dropped down at the foot of her grave as I opened my eyes. Tracing my fingers gently across the sand, I wrote:

Here lies my best friend and sister, Olivia, who was murdered by the powers and principalities.

I slowly got to my feet, taking it all in for a few more seconds. I glanced over my words and my sister's resting place one last time before stumbling away into the woods.

***

Bird chirps reached my ears as I stirred among the leaves. A drop of water landed on my cheek as I blinked open my eyes. I instantly wiped it away, sitting up as sunlight filtered through the trees. The night had come so fast that I decided to camp out among the trees. Although the scene was peaceful and I felt certain I was safe, sleep had been hard to come by. It had been a restless night full of tears and thinking of my sister. A certain stillness clung to the air and my whole body ached. The world felt so empty and strange. *What now, Lord?*

I rose to my feet, shaking off some leaves and blinking my heavy eyelids. My makeshift bed consisting of a pile of leaves had left me sore. Yawning, I stretched a bit as I took my first few steps. Each step felt so heavy against my raw feet. I had attempted to dry my shoes and socks off, but my shoes still had a damp feeling. My socks were a bit stiff and had an unpleasant odor, as did the rest of my clothes. I was eager to get out of them and wash up but had no clue how to get back to the pizzeria or Carlotta's group.

The group! The Uprising! The attack on the other station would have taken place by now. It hadn't even crossed my mind last night while I tossed and turned on leaves that somewhere out there another regulator station had been attacked. *If only they had come for our station!* We could have waited. In fact, we *would* have waited for them. I breathed sharply through my nose as I pondered how differently yesterday could have played out if they had gone after our station instead. *Would Olivia still be alive, if the Uprising had come for us? Could they have saved her?*

I shook the thoughts away. It was no use imagining the 'what ifs?' and I knew that realistically the same scenario might have still played out. I wandered through the trees as memories of the previous day played continuously in my mind. Hot tears streamed down my face as I pressed onward. I didn't even care to hold them back or hide them.

The birds hummed above me, completely oblivious to my circumstances. *Oh Lord, why can't this all be a bad dream? Why couldn't you have taken me instead? Why didn't you save her?* I wiped the tears away as the trees thinned out.

My stomach grumbled as I exited the woods and entered the city. I desperately needed to find food. As I started to jog down the paved, fancy streets of the neighborhood I now found myself in, I glanced back at the trees one last time. *Goodbye, Olivia.* Feeling a sudden rush of strength, I added, *Watch over me! I'm going to make you so proud.*

Chapter Seventeen

Harriet slammed a folder and book down on the table next to her water bottle. The meeting room began to fill with chatter as individuals entered the space. She glanced around as a few folks sat down in the black chairs bordering the long wooden table. As more and more tried to shuffle into the room, she let out a sigh and gathered her belongings back into her arms.

She moved through the crowd until she reached Dallas who at once turned to greet her. In his hand was a small cup with a dark brown liquid, presumably coffee.

"We need to move to a bigger space," Harriet said as he leaned closer. "There's too many people."

He glanced around the packed room, taking the folder and book into his arms. "What about the old gym? It's right down the hall."

Harriet nodded. "Go let the back of the crowd know. I'll meet you there."

Dallas dashed off at once while Harriet raised her voice to direct those gathered in the room to the new meeting location. Shortly after she gave the command, individuals filtered out the space, tucking in chairs as they got up. She escorted the crowd as they moved through the fallout shelter's hall, shuffling forward until they emerged into a large open space at the end of the hallway. The space contained a single basketball net along the wall with racks of sports balls underneath it. Shoes squeaked against the hard floor as individuals filled the space.

Harriet weaved through the mass of people, climbing onto a chair against the back wall so she could address her audience. She breathed out a sigh of relief as Dallas moved through the crowd to take his place at her side. As the noise died down and eyes turned to her, Harriet cleared her throat.

"Good evening!" She drew in a deep breath, clutching her water bottle tightly as a multitude of eyes rested on her. "Thank you all for making the journey to come here tonight to be part of this movement. This important work cannot be done without each of you and the unique gifts and skills you bring. With your help, we have grown from a small huddle of twelve to a number that rivals that of the emperor and his regulators, a number that has proven victorious! With your help, we have taken out a total of three regulator stations and have had successful protests throughout the city — many regulators have surrendered, fled into the wilderness, or retreated into Center City!" She paused briefly as cheers echoed through the space. She glanced over at Dallas, who returned her smile. After the noise died down, she raised her voice again. "I could not be prouder of this movement and all we've accomplished together. When humanity gathered in bunkers and fallout shelters at the height of the war, hope remained as a small still voice, speaking of a better future where all people could flourish and thrive in peace and fellowship. Now that small still voice lives on in each of you, burning for that better society we know is possible.

"The emperor thought he could kill that hope as nation after nation was wiped out, as his rivals were wiped out one by one. In the end, only he was left. For a moment, it appeared he had won. He held all the power and could rule however he wanted, with fear and force. That was until all of us rose up to challenge his power and principles.

"Our resistance against our common oppressor has proven successful and gained much momentum as our ranks continue to grow. Together, we are demonstrating we too are powerful. Together, we are showing we will not accept the status quo. Our movement serves as a powerful reminder that no human is unworthy to inherit the new earth. The emperor's plan to cleanse the population is shameful — to those of you who are disabled, know you are not unworthy. To those of you who are living with chronic pain or struggling with mental illness, know you are not unworthy. To those of you who worship someone other than the emperor, know you are not unworthy. To those of you who love the same gender, know you are not unworthy. To those of you living with disease, or sickness — all of you, know you are not unworthy." Her voice rose as cheers erupted from the crowd. "I am sure you all have heard by now of the horrible slaughter that took place the other night at station three. The emperor and his regulators want to convince the public these lives did not matter, that they were unworthy. But we know every life is infinitely valuable and *no one* is unworthy. We will not let their deaths be in vain!" The cheering got louder, prompting Harriet to take a break. As she glanced over the mass of people present, she felt herself relax. *These people believe in me and my abilities*, she realized. *They truly feel as strongly and as passionately as I do about making things right.* She took a quick sip of water before starting again. *How lucky I am to lead such a strong and brave group of revolutionaries!*

"Tomorrow night, we will honor those we've lost with action. We will gather in the woods across from station three right at dusk. After we gain the victory tomorrow, we will shift our focus to Center City. It's time for the government's headquarters to take a hit and be held accountable as well. So, rest up and prepare to channel your pain and anger into action. Train, uplift one another, and gather your weapons.

We *will* gain the victory and send a reminder to the emperor that hope is alive and burns strongly in those he has cast out. We *will* overcome, and I look forward to fighting alongside you all tomorrow night. Take care beloveds, and keep your hope alive and burning!"

The crowd roared and cheered as Harriet concluded her speech. As she stepped off the chair and sprinted to Dallas, she couldn't hold back her smile.

"I told you you'd do great!" he greeted her. "If I got up there, and saw all those people watching me, my mind would have completely gone blank! I don't know how you do it."

"I'm sure you could come up with some random fact or joke to break the awkward silence," Harriet teased her friend as they exited the room.

"Hey, that's a great idea!" Dallas perked up. "Maybe I should start the next meeting with a joke!"

Harriet shook her head, giggling slightly to please her friend. The two swapped lame jokes as they continued down the halls. The jokes lifted her spirit a bit, and Harriet felt certain that no matter what tomorrow night would bring, she and Dallas would be ready to face it and bring about the change they had been fighting for since their youth.

Chapter Eighteen

I let out a yawn as I stretched on the old pizza booth that had become my bed. Slowly rising to my feet, I approached the large kitchen sink, letting it run for only a couple seconds before washing my face.

I shut it off instantly, breathing deeply as I dried my face on a nearby towel. I *despised* the sound of rushing water. It brought back memories of the roaring river that stole my sister from me. I could still picture her lifeless body pinned against the rock and the loud bangs that erupted from the regulator's guns. The memory of that day remained clear as the passing weeks evolved into months.

I not only lost track of time in the months since Olivia's death, but also my inner compass when I trekked into the city. I never traveled far from the pizzeria anymore. The streets in this part of town were now as familiar to me as the back of my hand, but beyond that, I didn't care to explore more ruins and especially did not want to wander around any populated regions out of fear the regulators might recognize me.

As I got dressed for the day, my mind drifted to Carlotta and her group. *Are they safe?* I wondered. *Do they still participate in Uprising attacks?* I thought about Carlotta's friendly green eyes and Elliot's warm smile. Despite not knowing any of them well, a yearning had blossomed within me in recent days to visit them again. I had searched desperately to find their hideout again, but with no luck. *I hope they don't think Olivia and I completely abandoned them!*

As I thought about my sister, my gaze landed on her stack of clothes. On top rested a hairbrush and the barrettes she wore on her final day. Two barrettes had flowers at their tips while the other was adorned with a butterfly. I tucked the barrettes safely into my pocket before heading toward the kitchen door.

I sighed as I slipped on my shoes and grabbed a crumpled up plastic bag. It was old and contained a few holes, but it was all I had. I didn't *want* to leave the pizzeria, but I knew I had to. I was in desperate need of more food. Tucking the bag into my pocket, I set out into the streets.

The outside world was silent. The few people I came across hurried from one building to the next. I forged onward as a hot breeze stung my exposed face. As soon as an alleyway came into view, I ducked into it and raced to the nearest dumpster. After ensuring the coast was clear, I quietly filled my bag with food.

I moved from dumpster to dumpster, salvaging what I could. As my fingers shifted through the last pile of rubbish, I felt the urge to cry.

It had become nearly impossible to dumpster dive for long. After stashing away the rest of the good food I spotted, I rushed out of the alleyway. Quickening my pace, I belted back into the abandoned suburbs as I fought my tears. The old houses blended together as water blurred my vision. *Oh, why did we not dumpster dive in a different alleyway that day? Why did things have to happen the way they did?*

I turned a street corner as memories of my final day with Olivia began to surface. The tears I tried so hard to hold back now poured down my face. I could still picture her smile so clearly, and memories of us playing and joking around filled my mind. *Oh, Olivia! How I miss you so!*

Wiping my eyes, I glanced around. I had run farther than I'd intended. As I looked around the unfamiliar street nervously, I caught sight of movement. Someone was crossing between the houses farther down the road. They continued in the opposite direction, presumably unaware of my presence. Gripping my bag tightly and wiping away more tears, I dashed off in their direction.

I was careful to not make any noise as I trailed behind them. They walked on, completely oblivious of me. Their hair was bundled up into a hat, which was the only part of their outfit not torn or covered in patches. They looked well fed, and I prayed they would lead me somewhere flowing with food.

I licked my lips as they pulled a bright red apple out of their pocket. As I walked a few steps closer, a crackling noise played under my feet. I froze in my tracks while the stranger spun around to face me. I moved my foot off the tree branch, my pulse quickening. *Oh no*, I thought, shrinking back. *What if they're a bad person? What if they're with the regulators and get me locked up again? Why didn't I consider all the possibilities before following them?*

My worry faded once they removed their sunglasses and hat. A smile crept across my lips as the familiar face came closer.

"Oliver? That's your name, isn't it?"

"Kailey!" I wiped my eyes, hoping all my tears were gone.

She relaxed her shoulders. "Oh, thank goodness! You startled me!" She took another bite of her apple.

"Sorry about that." I blushed, casting my gaze downward. I slowly brought my gaze back up to meet hers. "It's just been so long! How is everyone?"

"We've been doing great!" she said as the two of us started walking side by side. "Truly, the crew's all well. Although being inside and well stocked helps out a lot, don't you think?"

I smiled, glad to finally have company after so many days alone. "It's been too hot to go outside."

"Tell me about it!" Kailey's voice took on a playful tone. "None of us want to go outside, not even Husker. I lost the bet so I'm out here now gathering supplies."

"I'll go with you!" I offered, thankful when she didn't object.

The two of us moved swiftly through the abandoned streets. I completely lost all sense of direction, but Kailey strode onward, her back straight and head held high. It was as if she had no fear of the regulators. She placed her sunglasses and hat back on as we approached a busy street, tossing the core of her apple in a nearby trash can. We at once started to walk like the city folks.

"So," I said as we turned down a busy street. "How long have you been with the group?"

"A little over a year. Chester came across me one night as I was sleeping behind a dumpster. He found me about a week after Meemaw died." She paused briefly. "Anyways, once Chester found out I was lost and alone, he invited me to join. How could I resist?" She let out a laugh. "I could barely fend for myself and was starving! I don't think I would have lasted much longer out on the streets."

I shifted closer to her. "I'm sorry about your Meemaw, and I'm glad Chester found you when he did. Living alone on the streets isn't easy. I have no idea how I've been managing so long now on my own."

Kailey stopped, turned abruptly to meet my gaze. "Alone? What do you mean? Do you and your sister not live together anymore?"

My gaze dropped as did my stomach. I had known this conversation was inevitable, but still I felt ill-prepared. I reached my hand into my pocket, tightly holding one of the barrettes as my lip quivered. "Olivia's, um . . . she's not around anymore. The regulators killed her. We tried to get back to you all, but they caught us." Feeling a lump in my throat, I squeezed my eyes shut to avoid tears.

I felt Kailey's hand rest gently on my shoulder. "Oh, Oliver. I'm so sorry." The two of us embraced in a hug, causing me to remove my hand from my pocket and release the grip I had on the barrettes. "Please know me, Carlotta, and Chester — *all* of us are here if you need anything."

"Thank you." My voice cracked as I pulled away.

The two of us began to walk slowly, not saying much else. I knew if I tried to say more, the tears would flow again. I breathed deeply, doing my best to shift my mind away from Olivia and to the present. Kailey's small smiles and friendly side glances helped as we continued.

"The store up here gets rid of so much," Kailey whispered as we turned down an alleyway. "Fingers crossed they'll have what I need."

"What kind of store is it?" I asked, thankful for the new conversation.

"I think it's an old pharmacy. They have a little bit of everything." Kailey crouched down beside some stacked boxes. Taking out a small knife, she opened the box nearest to her. I glanced around anxiously as she did so.

She moved quickly through the boxes. "I've got to find some bandages and cream. Trevor has a nasty injury that needs patching up."

"Is he okay?" I asked, crouching down near her. *The attack!* I suddenly remembered. "Did he get hurt when you all attacked the regulator station? What was that like?"

"Loud!" Kailey responded, pulling open a box. "The Uprising took out most of the building with grenades and set the rest on fire. We gave those bastards a good run, and some even surrendered." She paused, digging through the box contents. "But no, Trevor just got a little scratched up from playing with stray kittens."

I managed a small smile, peering into a box full of canned vegetables. "Sounds like it went well then," I said, scooping a few of the cans into my bag.

"Yes, very well!" Kailey ripped open a smaller box. "Bingo!" she said, stuffing some of the contents into her pockets before closing the box and setting it aside. She then climbed to her feet and backed away from the area. I followed, eager to get out of the alley.

"So," Kailey started, the two of us hurrying down the street as the wind picked up. "How do you spend your days now? What kind of things do you do? You know, when you're not in the city gathering supplies."

"Oh, um . . ." *I can't tell her I spend most of my time sleeping and gathering food! That's not exciting!* "I enjoy going for walks! A bit dangerous, but helps to take my mind off things."

"I get that. For me personally, reading helps a lot. Helps me escape this awful world and enter a much better one!"

"What have you been reading recently?" It had been a while since I last read anything. I especially missed reading my pocket Bible.

"I've been reading this fantasy novel. It has dragons and castles and all sorts of cool things! I haven't been able to read it these past few days though, because they killed off my favorite character. Just hasn't been the same." She paused briefly as we turned a corner. "And like her death was *so* unnecessary and *so* rude and stupid! And then her best friend gets with her boyfriend and they, you know . . ." She trailed off with a smirk.

"Know what?"

"Things get really spicy . . . like super spicy!"

"They what!?"

She grinned, holding back laughter. "You don't know?"

"Well, I might know if you tell me." I gave a weak smile, switching my bag to my other arm.

"No!" She was barely able to hold back her laughter at this point. "You'll figure it out eventually. Besides," she came to a stop. "This is where I found you."

The two of us stayed silent for a bit, glancing at one another and also the abandoned homes that surrounded us.

"I, I do need to get back now." Kailey finally broke the silence. She placed her hand gently on my shoulder. "And please, Oliver, take care of yourself. Stay indoors and stay cool. I hope to see you around more."

I nodded as she removed her hand, giving me a small wave goodbye before turning to leave. I felt my stomach churn as she took the first few steps away from me. I took a step forward, my mind the clearest it had been in weeks. I knew exactly what I wanted and exactly what to do.

"Wait!" I called out. "Take me with you!"

Chapter Nineteen

"Oliver? You've come back?" Carlotta asked, racing to meet Kailey and me as we entered the cool basement. In her hands were two large wooden needles covered with purple yarn. Her fingers glided effortlessly as the needles clicked together, though what she was knitting, I could not tell. Not even as she came closer.

"If it's okay, I'd love to stay here again." I quickly added, "I wanted to get back to you all sooner, but couldn't find the way." Sid, the twins, and Max glanced up from the bean bag chairs as I answered. *I feel so good*, I realized as I met their friendly gazes. *This is the best I've felt in a long while!*

Carlotta smiled, her eyes just as bright and friendly as I remembered. "Well, we are pretty hidden! And of course you're welcome to stay." I felt my heart soar at her words. She turned to Kailey who pulled the items we'd gathered out of her pockets. "You find anything out there?"

"Found exactly what we needed!" Kailey beamed as Chester poked his head out of Trevor's room. He flashed me a smile before ducking back in. Kailey stepped into the room, shutting the door behind her.

Carlotta turned to me, continuing to knit. "Are you hungry? Thirsty?"

I shook my head. "I appreciate it, but I'm okay."

"Well, make yourself at home!" Carlotta said. "We've been taking things easy around here and mostly just trying to stay cool."

I nodded in response as she turned to head up the stairs. I slowly approached the bean bag area. The members smiled at me as Jennifer bounded toward my direction.

"Oliver!" Her eyes sparkled above her wide smile. She wrapped her arms around my waist. "We've missed you!"

I hugged her back. "I missed you all too!"

She let go, racing back to her spot next to Annie who nodded to acknowledge me. Max glanced up from his book, his eyes locked on me as I crossed the space to Sid, who was drawing away in a large notebook. *It's only fair to tell her*, I thought. She and Olivia grew close during our short stay here. *That way she'll know Olivia didn't just ditch their friendship.*

"Hello Sid." I took a seat in the bean bag across from her, setting my bag down beside me. She glanced up, dropping her pen into her lap.

"It's good to see you again, Oliver." Her brown eyes examined my face as if searching for answers. I felt my heart sink. *She must be wondering about Olivia's whereabouts,* I assumed.

"Sid," I gulped, reaching into my pocket and taking out the barrettes she'd let Olivia borrow. She leaned forward as I did so, carefully taking the barrettes into her own palm. "I've got some bad news. It's about Olivia." I drew in a deep breath before continuing. "Olivia . . . she didn't make it one night . . . the regulators were shooting at us, and they got her . . ." My voice shook as I felt an empty pit in my stomach. I turned away briefly, scrunching up my face. Sid looked away as well.

"Thank you for telling me," she said softly after a moment of heavy silence. She hugged me gently before leaning back in the old bean bag chair. "I know I didn't know her well, but I could tell Olivia was a good soul. I'll never forget her." She picked her pen back up and turned her attention once more to the open notebook, flipping to a blank page. "Maybe I'll draw something for her next."

I watched as she placed the barrettes down beside her. It felt like someone was tugging at my heart, especially as I noticed a strand of blond hair stuck in one. *What's she going to do with them?*

Sid glanced up, pausing from her work to follow my gaze. "Oh," she whispered softly, picking them back up. "I'm sure it's hard to let go of things that remind you of her." The barrettes clicked as she held out her palm. "Would you like to hold on to one for a while?"

I nodded, taking the butterfly clip that had Olivia's hair still stuck in it.

"Thanks," I whispered.

"Of course."

Sid turned back to her drawing as I stirred to my feet and grabbed my bag. I tucked the hair accessory into my pocket, forcing a smile as Jennifer and Annie came to my side.

"You can stay down here with us, Oliver!" Jennifer said, her eyes bright. "We've got some cozy blankets and lots of pillows for you!"

Max rolled his eyes. "Oh, please." He placed a pen into the book he was reading. "Every piece of furniture down here is taken."

"Yeah, but Annie and I could share or someone could move or—"

"There's *no* way you two are going to share," Max chuckled. "You two fight worse than cats and dogs!" Max turned his gaze to me. "Oliver, why don't you check upstairs? After all, Elliot has a whole room to himself. I'm sure he wouldn't mind giving up a corner."

"Um, sure!" Jennifer glared at Max as I spoke. "Sorry girls," I said to the twins as I exited the space and climbed the steps.

The upstairs was a tad bit warmer, but still comfortable. I moved quickly down the old hall, yearning to find Elliot. I had missed the boy and his witty jokes and random facts about technology. After setting my bag on the kitchen table, I bounded off toward Elliot's room.

Elliot sat against the wall, the old laptop resting on his lap. He continued staring down at the screen as I entered the space.

"I told you, Chester, I'm not going out in this weather. Besides, Kailey lost the bet! Tell her—" He paused, his eyes widening and a smile spreading across his lips as he glanced up from the screen to find me, not Chester, in his room. Setting the laptop down, he climbed to his feet and rushed toward me.

"Oliver!" He threw his arms around me in a hug. I hugged him back, feeling a smile stretch across my face as well. "It's so good to see you!"

"It's good to see you too!" I cheerfully said as Elliot pulled away, his face still lit with a warm smile. All the members of the group had such contagious smiles but Elliot's in particular was so warm.

Elliot took a few steps back to the laptop, motioning for me to follow. "Look!" He scooped up the computer. "There's still no signal, but I got some games up and running!" He clicked across the bottom of the screen, which caused the device to show a green screen with some cards.

"Incredible," I said as Elliot placed the laptop on the table in the center of the room.

He glanced back at me, his face glowing. "I know, right? So anyways, how have you been? *Where* have you been?"

His expression changed from excitement to shock to surprise as I told him all about the regulators and how they had taken us.

"What?" His jaw dropped. "Wait, so the people who freed you all, they were just others being held there? That definitely would have thrown me off as well! But I'm glad you all got free!"

"Yes, and thank you!" I glanced around nervously, debating how to share the next part of the story. "Elliot, there's something I need to tell you." I raised my gaze to meet his dark brown eyes. "I've only told a few others, because it's hard to talk about. While we were running out of the station and the regulators were shooting us . . ." Elliot's eyes were still friendly, but I caught a glimpse of uncertainty as I trailed off. *Oh no*, I thought, my lip quivering. *I can't cry. Not here. Not now.* I swallowed before starting again, reaching my hand down to rest over my pocket containing the barrette. "Some of the bullets hit Olivia. She . . . she didn't make it." I paused, blinking fast to hold back tears. Elliot's eyes were soft and locked on me.

"Oh Oliver," he said. "I'm so, so sorry. I can't even imagine how hard that must have been — to witness *and* deal with in the following days and weeks. I'm sure Olivia's absence leaves a hole that can't be filled. Thank you for sharing with me, and for trusting me with your story. If you don't mind me asking, and you certainly don't have to answer this, where did you bury her, if you even did?"

I breathed in deeply to regulate my stirring grief. "I appreciate it. I buried her alongside the others who were shot and killed, down by the river."

"Oh, good." Elliot's voice was soft. "I wanted to check because there's this really pretty spot not too far where we buried one of our group members, someone who didn't survive the first Uprising attack we joined. I wanted to make sure Olivia had a good resting spot."

I raised an eyebrow. "There were others? I mean, before I came across you all?"

"Oh, um yeah." Elliot tucked some of his hair behind his ear, casting his gaze downward. "I'm not sure I should have mentioned it, but I already did." He grinned slightly but quickly dropped it as he continued. "During the first Uprising attack we joined, Jordyn got badly injured. Shot quite a lot. Max and I tried to carry her back home, but she didn't make it." He paused, his voice growing soft. "Carlotta's never been the same since. The two of them were good friends."

I felt sick at Elliot's words. *How many have the regulators killed? What if they get me next, or Elliot, or the twins, or Kailey, or all of us?* I shivered at the thought.

"But hey," Elliot met my gaze, his tone more cheerful. "We're both here, safe and alive. Now we get to fight in memory of them. And really just live each day for them. I don't know about you, but I want to make sure neither of them died in vain."

I nodded, not sure what to say.

"So," he said, closing the laptop. "Where have you been staying? Back at the pizzeria?"

"Yes!" I was thankful for the conversation change. "That's actually what I came up here for. They didn't have space for me downstairs, so I came to inquire about staying up here."

Elliot's eyes lit up. "I'd love that!" He glanced around the space. "I sleep over there," he pointed to the area he had been sitting previously, an area lined with some blankets and pillows. "But you're free to set up wherever. We've got plenty of extra pillows and blankets. The house came with them."

I looked around the space that was littered with pillows and blankets. "That would be awesome!" I said, trying to determine which part of the room would be most comfortable.

"Plus, there's food right around the corner if you want a late-night snack. Less noise at night too, no one chit-chatting. As long as you don't mind my snoring or kickin'!"

I chuckled. "Not at all!"

"Do you have anything back at the pizzeria we need to go get? I know you caught me saying I was not going out in this weather, but I'll go if you need help."

I nodded. "Actually, I do need to go get my things. It's not much, and I would appreciate the help."

Elliot smiled. "I'll go get my shoes on then. Come on!" He cheerfully skipped to the room's entrance. "They're by the back door."

I swiftly followed, feeling hope and excitement rise within me. I was not sure what my future held, but I was thrilled to have companionship once again as I faced it.

Chapter Twenty

"Good morning sleepyhead!"

I blinked open my eyes, yawning as I sat up. The mound of blankets and pillows I had compiled into a bed was *much* more comfortable than the pizzeria booths. I smiled, rising to my feet and heading toward my pile of belongings in the corner. It had been the first night I had slept peacefully since Olivia's death.

"How long have you been up?" I asked Elliot, who munched away on a piece of bread near the room's entrance.

"Only about ten minutes," Elliot answered between bites. I flipped through my clothes, pulling out a clean outfit for the day. "Don't worry," he grinned. "Plenty of the others are still snoozing."

"Well, I'd love to see who's up after I get ready!"

Elliot chuckled, turning to leave the room. "Don't take too long!"

I quickly changed into a white tee and black cargo shorts, both hand-me-downs from Chester. They were a little big on me, but I was thankful for new clothes. Many of mine were starting to tear after so much use. I was also grateful for the opportunity yesterday to bathe and wash my clothes in the bathroom tub. My new outfit felt soft against my clean skin.

Tucking Olivia's barrette into my pocket, I emerged from the dark room into the sun-filled kitchen. Elliot leaned up against the center table, chewing away on the same piece of bread. I headed toward the sink, reaching for my cup.

"How was your first night?" Elliot asked as I filled my cup with water. "Did you sleep okay?"

"Like a log! What about you?"

"I slept great!" Elliot said as he finished the slice of bread. He wiped his hands against his pajama pants as I took a few sips from my cup. The water soothed my dry throat and after finishing my last gulp, I put it back down with the other cups and gave Elliot a smile.

"Okay, I'm ready now!"

The two of us headed out the kitchen, down the hall, and descended the stairs. As we leaped off the final step, Chester and Max glanced up from where they leaned against the wall. Beyond them, other members rested on top of bean bag chairs or the bunk beds except for Husker who lay peacefully on the couch.

Carlotta was also up, strolling around Jennifer and Annie. The twins lay stretched out across the bean bag chairs, chatting.

"Come on, girls!" She whispered to them. "If you're up, get some food and water in your bellies. We've got another hot day ahead." The twins groaned, remaining in their spots. Carlotta's gaze met mine and she quickly approached us as we came to where Chester and Max stood.

"Good morning!" Carlotta said, keeping her voice low. "Oliver, feel free to help yourself to some breakfast. We have plenty upstairs."

"Thank you. Is there anything you all need help with?" I wasn't very hungry after last night's dinner but was eager to give back however I could.

Chester shook his head. "No, but thank you Oliver. We've got some books and games if you're looking for something to do."

"You don't happen to have a Bible, do you?" I glanced at the books lining the shelves above the bean bag chairs. I yearned to read, especially after yesterday's conversation with Kailey.

"I'm sorry, Oliver," Max spoke up. "I've been searching for one myself but haven't come across any. Not even at the library ruins."

"What about the abandoned church?" Elliot's question made me perk up. *There's a church?* I imagined a gorgeous building with a tall steeple and beautiful stained-glass windows, similar to the ones the adults at the orphanage described from memory. *The regulators left one standing?* The emperor had quickly ordered places of worship to be demolished shortly after the war. It seemed odd he would leave any standing, especially with laws claiming only he was to be worshipped.

"There's an abandoned church?" Carlotta furrowed her brows. "Where?"

"Just beyond one of the busy streets, tucked behind some trees," Elliot explained. "It's not far from the farm."

Max leaned closer to Elliot with wide eyes. "Can you show me where? If you don't mind the heat that is."

"I'd like to go, too!" I blurted out.

"Okay! But let me get dressed first."

"If you're headed that way, can you all please grab some food?" Carlotta asked. "It would be good to stock up and for Oliver to get acquainted with the farm."

Max nodded. "We'll be sure to."

I watched Elliot bound up the stairs. "You all don't have a spare bag I can borrow, do you? I brought a bag with me last night, but it's starting to fall apart. I'd hate for it to rip through."

"You can borrow one of mine," Max said, taking a few steps toward the bunk bed area. "I have extra."

"Okay," I said, quietly following Max to the bunk beds. I still wasn't sure what to think of the boy. At times he seemed friendly, but other times he seemed distant and cold. *Please don't be in a bad mood today,* I thought as we entered the bunk bed area.

A few of the group members snored softly in their beds while someone on a top bunk rolled over. *They're so much quieter than Elliot!* I thought with a smile. Surprisingly, I didn't mind his snores too much. They reminded me of being back at the orphanage, surrounded by adults who snored louder than a chainsaw.

Max crouched down and reached under one of the bunk beds. He pulled out two white mesh bags, handing one to me. We slung the bags across our shoulders as we headed to the back door. Elliot slipped into boots as we came to his side. He wore camouflage shorts and a stained white tee. On top his head was a brown cap.

"Don't say I never did nothin' for you!" Elliot joked as we slid on our own shoes. He tucked his hair into his hat, wrapping a red scarf around his face. *Perhaps Carlotta made him that,* I thought as I noticed the scarf was made from the same yarn she knitted with.

"You all be careful!" Carlotta called from where she and Chester leaned near Trevor's door. I nodded in their direction, then set out with my two companions into the blazing heat.

***

Elliot led us through the abandoned neighborhood into a crowded part of town. As we approached the busy streets, Max pulled a beanie and sunglasses out of his pocket, quickly putting them on. He handed a second pair of sunglasses to Elliot.

"You're lucky you don't have to hide your features," Elliot said to me, adjusting the glasses securely against his face.

"I suppose I did get lucky," I muttered as the three of us began to walk like the city folks. Despite the brutal wind and high temperature, plenty of people were out and about.

"The trick is making sure you put them on in time," Elliot added. "And don't get near any regulators or they'll want you to take your hat and glasses off."

"You sure do look like them, boy," Max remarked, his eyes narrowing as he glanced me over. He had been watching me closely as we trekked through the city, but looked away quickly whenever I met his gaze.

Not this again, I thought as I pressed my lips together and shot a glance at Max. He instantly turned away. *Why can't he let it go?* I felt my shoulders tense up. *Why can't he drop these silly accusations?*

Before I could respond, Elliot lightly slapped the back of Max's head. "Lay off my new roomie, will ya? He hasn't done anything wrong, and I can tell he isn't going to." Elliot's tone was soft but also firm. With a chuckle, he added, "Do you really think I'd let him sleep in my room if not?"

Max smirked as if amused. "We'll see how this plays out." Without another word, he quickened his pace to take the lead as we turned down another street.

"Try not to take it too personally," Elliot whispered to me. "He's always been wary of newcomers. Give him a couple more weeks and he'll come around. Dumb rascal was afraid of me too when I first joined. After all," he snickered. "I just have to dye my hair and put in some contacts, and I'd look like the city folks too."

I managed a small chuckle, my shoulders and face starting to relax. I adored my new roomie.

"Elliot!" Max called out from a few steps ahead. "How much farther do we have to go?"

Elliot sprinted to catch up with him, me right on his tail. "We're getting close! Trust me, I'm not planning to be out in this weather any longer than necessary."

The three of us continued, cutting through side streets and leaping over potholes. Eventually, the streets became rough with cracks and overgrown weeds and the decrepit homes I had grown used to. I felt thankful that Max stopped watching me the farther we traveled.

"It amazes me how wrecked some neighborhoods are," I said as we stepped over a crumbling sidewalk. "Like, I thought no nukes dropped on us! But it looks that way, and I can't help but wonder where all the people went."

"We didn't get blasted," Max responded. He sounded slightly irritated. "But the country north of us did, to smithereens. We got a *lot* of their radiation and soot. If you weren't already underground back then, well, you were basically screwed. Most people on the surface got sick and passed away, especially without food. These homes they left behind have been abandoned for over a decade now. This is how buildings look when there's no one around to care for them."

"Didn't the Uprising also clash with regulators in neighborhoods, when they first started to organize?" Elliot chimed in. "I thought I heard about that. It would explain why some homes look the way they do, all wrecked and all."

"Oh, right. That did happen to many—"

Before Max could complete his sentence, a yell pierced through the air. I jumped as the three of us froze in our tracks.

"Look!" Max pointed past the homes. My heart sank once I caught a glimpse of vivid orange flames rising above the trees.

"Looks like they're burning down another building," Elliot whispered, the three of us staring intently at the bright fire. "Quick! The church is this way."

We hurried into the barren trees behind the homes. I glanced back frequently, dumbfounded as the flames engulfed one of the houses.

"Won't the fire spread?" I asked, dodging under a low-hanging branch.

"Nah, the regulators control it," Max said from a few steps ahead. "They burn down any building they believe the Uprising is using."

I slowed my steps briefly as Max's words sunk in, my mind recalling the old house Olivia and I had explored. I thought about the locked doors, the leftover food, and the certainty of the cats. *Perhaps you were on to something, Olivia,* I thought. It all started to click as I remembered how only a few of the houses were burnt down while others had been left untouched. I felt crestfallen as I connected the dots. *That old house* was *being used!* I shook the memory away, bounding once again after Max and Elliot as the trees grew thicker.

After a few more minutes, we emerged onto a gravel parking lot. Up ahead a gravel road led even deeper into the trees. Off in the distance I caught sight of a crumbling house along the old road. Trees engulfed the area.

I drew in a sharp breath as I gazed at the beautiful gray stone structure before us. It was small with a side crumbling in, similar to the pizzeria. The side still intact was lined with multiple colorful windows, the sun reflecting beautifully off the various shades. At the front of the building stood large, wooden double doors, and above that a steeple reached for the sky. It was much more beautiful than anything I'd envisioned in my mind.

"Pretty cool, huh?" Elliot said, taking a few steps toward the church.

"It sure is exciting!" Max exclaimed.

"So glad they missed one," I said, glancing around briefly before crossing the gravel, eager to discover how the inside looked. After all, I'd imagined this moment many times since converting to Christianity!

Chapter Twenty-One

The inside of the church was just as stunning with warm red carpet and white dazzling walls. Multiple rows of wooden pews filled the space, leading to a raised wooden chancel. On the right side of the chancel was a podium and in the middle was a wooden table with a large open book stretched across it. The space was illuminated with rainbow light from the stained-glass windows.

"Oh, wow!" Max breathed out as we approached the chancel. "This is beautiful!"

A breeze stirred in from outside, making me feel light as I imagined the place full of believers worshipping and praising the Lord God. I pictured them with all sorts of hair colors. Some wore the same ragged clothes as us. A smile crept across my face as they raised their hands in song.

"Oliver, this is a Bible!" Elliot called out excitingly as he flipped through the large book on the table. I turned my attention back to the present, quickly bounding up to Elliot's side. Sure enough, the huge book was Holy Scripture, opened to the Gospel of John.

"Maybe there's a smaller one somewhere," Max spoke up as he walked along the back of the chancel. With a smirk, he added, "It would be a bit hard to carry that one back."

I glanced around. "I'll search through the pews."

Elliot joined me as the two of us combed through the aisles, looking under and around the long pews. Max continued to search around the chancel, finding hymnal books tucked under a few chairs but no Bibles. Elliot and I eventually rejoined him, our hands empty.

The three of us walked down the aisle without a word. I could feel the defeat lingering in the air. As Max and I walked the pews one last time, Elliot bounded off to the edge of the chancel where the wall crumbled away. I watched him intently as he called for us to come closer.

"There's more behind here!" Elliot said, stepping over the rubble. Max and I followed closely, the three of us emerging through a small crack into an area behind the church. Other than three closed doors and a rack of church robes, the space was empty.

"Great catch, Elliot!" Max said as he tried the first door. It refused to open. I turned the golden handle of the second door as Elliot moved to the third. Mine also refused to budge.

"Got it!" Elliot said as he pushed open the last door. We peered into the dark space, assuming it was once an office due to the desk and chair, which took up nearly the entire room. Papers were scattered across the desk along with some books. Very little light filtered in from closed window blinds.

"This room is tiny," Elliot remarked.

Max held out his arms, nearly touching the wall on either side. "I'd say only a few feet."

"It's *got* to be more than that," Elliot said, beginning to walk slowly through the space, one foot directly in front of the other. He started to cross the room in a linear line, carefully lining up each step and counting out loud.

"That's not how it works," Max scoffed with a smile. "The system doesn't go off your feet, silly."

I picked a book off the desk, wiping away the dust while my two companions continued to banter. As I blew dust off a second book, a screech from Elliot pierced through the stale air, causing Max and me to jump. I grabbed onto the desk for support while my heart leaped in my chest.

"There's . . . there's a body," Elliot breathed out, returning quickly to our side. I wrapped my arms around my friend as he hugged me tight. His racing heart pounded against my chest.

Max slowly walked around the desk, stooping down slightly. I gradually let go of Elliot and the book I was inspecting, staggering around the desk myself. Burying multiple people, including my sister, had made me numb to corpses. I felt certain I could handle the scene.

Behind the desk, face down on the ground, was a tall man. His church robes completely covered him, except his ghostly pale bald head and outstretched hands, one of which clutched a piece of paper. His body showed little decay, and I guessed he hadn't been deceased for long.

I hunched down near the pastor's side. *What happened to you? I wondered,* leaning closer. I didn't see any signs of trauma. As my eyes focused on the man, I thought about how much love he must have poured into this church. *Who were you? Why are you dead?* I continued to stare at the deceased man. A shiver ran down my spine as I pictured regulators finding the believer, shooting him, and shutting down the church. *But why would they leave the church standing and not burn it down?* I struggled to make sense of the situation.

Glancing closer at the piece of paper in his hands, I whispered out the scribbled words: "Father, do not hold this sin against them."

"That's the same thing Saint Stephen said before he was martyred," Max said, slowly moving away from the body. I remained where I was, saying a short silent prayer for the pastor. My mind drifted to the possibility of him meeting up with the saint now in Heaven. *Perhaps the guy Olivia and I saw getting hanged is with them, too*, I thought. They were all martyrs to me.

"I'm sorry for bringing you all here." Elliot cast his gaze to the ground as I stood back up. "If I had known, I wouldn't have done it."

I stepped carefully over the pastor's body. "Hey, you didn't know. It's not your fault."

"Besides," Max said as he looked over the books. "You led us to some Bibles."

I perked up as I came to Max's side. Sure enough, the words 'Holy Bible' in gold font were printed on some of the black books. *Yes!* I thought, picking up one of the Bibles. After flipping through the pages, I pulled the Bible close to my heart.

"Great, so we can leave now?" I could tell from the tone of Elliot's question the body deeply disturbed him.

"Definitely." Max placed two of the Bibles into the mesh bag slung across his shoulder. I tucked mine into my bag as well. Elliot quickly dashed out of the room, Max and I trailing behind him.

"You ready to gather some fresh food?" Max asked me as we exited the church.

"Certainly," I said, the three of us entering the bright, sunny outdoors once again.

***

"So, you've never been to a farm before?"

I shook my head at Elliot's question. "I've heard about them, but no. We relied on the underground greenhouse and canned food back at the orphanage."

"The one we go to is a small farm, but they're good folks who always have an abundance to share," Max said from a few steps ahead. "You'll like them."

The three of us strolled down winding streets as yards grew larger and fenced in fields began to surround us. Rows of crops lined the fields. In the distance, I caught sight of small red barns, greenhouses, and cattle resting. A few stone cottages were scattered about, some with tables around them. As we got closer, I noticed a few individuals moving through the fields, their hair pulled up and their clothes stained with mud. Freckles covered their tanned skin. I counted seven of them moving boxes from the tables to one of the barns.

Max and Elliot removed their sunglasses and hats as we approached the people, who waved cheerfully at us. A chicken also approached us before dashing away.

"We don't have to hide ourselves here," Elliot mentioned to me as he tucked his red scarf into his pocket.

I glanced at my friend's unique curls as they wrapped around his ears. "I wish you all never had to hide." It hurt watching my friends hide their gorgeous hair and bright eyes behind sunglasses and caps in busy parts of town. *You all deserve to wear your hair how you want it,* I thought as I glanced over my friends. *You all deserve to be free too — to let your hair hang loose like mine if you want.* At least they could be fully free back at the house and drop their disguises in places like this.

"Welcome!" A woman wearing a large sun hat greeted us with a wide smile as we gathered around a table containing open boxes and some sandwiches. Wrinkles curved around her friendly eyes.

"Hello, Martha," Max smiled. "This is Oliver, he's been staying with us for a bit."

"Good to meet you," I said, shaking her hand.

"You too. Boys, we have plenty. Please help yourselves." Another farmer came to greet us, carrying a box of dirt-covered potatoes. He placed them gently on the table, smiling and nodding at us before disappearing back into the field.

"How much for those?" I asked, pointing to the potatoes.

Max and Elliot chuckled, glancing away to hide their laughter. Martha just smiled.

"Oh sweetheart, don't worry about that! The Lord blessed us with a large harvest to share. Take what you need and leave what you don't."

I beamed at the mention of the Lord. Martha returned my smile before re-entering the nearest barn as we started to pick from the produce and eggs.

As I packed my bag to the brim and ate one of the sandwiches, a warm satisfaction spread through me. I was not only excited to get back to the group and feast, but also feeling deeply inspired. *Please Lord, let me model the kindness of these Christian farmers in the days to come!*

Chapter Twenty-Two

We plopped our stuffed bags onto the kitchen counter, the three of us sighing in exhaustion. The twins raced to us as we did so. Carlotta rushed to us as well, putting her knitting project down on the table. Chester glanced up from where he leaned against the sink. Various tools were scattered around him.

"What all did you get?" Jennifer asked, attempting to peek into the bags. Elliot tilted one of the bags slightly as she and Annie peered inside on their tippy-toes.

"Any eggs?" Annie asked.

"There's some in my bag," Max answered, taking a seat at the kitchen table. He exhaled deeply as he relaxed his shoulders and propped his feet up.

"Oh, this is great," Carlotta said as she and Elliot began removing the produce from the bags. I stepped forward to help, being extra careful as I laid each and every vegetable on the counter. Annie and Jennifer inspected each piece we pulled out before dashing to the sink to rinse off the vegetables.

"Elliot," Carlotta added as she carefully set the eggs on the table. "Go ahead and get some water boiling."

"On it!" The boy responded after the two of us had emptied the bags. I followed him as he pulled two large pots and a muffin pan out of a cabinet.

"What can I do to help?" I asked as he set the cookware on the counter. Chester pushed the tools to the side to create some space for Elliot.

"The sink shouldn't be leaking anymore," Chester said, watching the water intently as the twins washed up the produce.

"That's great! You got it all fixed up?" Elliot asked, then turning to me, added, "There's some tea light candles and matches in that top shelf." He motioned toward a cabinet in the corner. "Light a few and bring them over please."

I nodded, quickly heading to the cabinet. I pulled it open as Elliot and Chester continued to chat while Elliot filled the pots with water. Not sure how many they needed; I grabbed a handful of the candles and brought the entire box of matches to them.

"Do you know how to light them?" Chester asked as I reached their side. When I shook my head, he quickly stepped up, gently guiding me through the process.

I beamed as the match lit then started to light the candles, feeling a sense of accomplishment as I did so.

"Perfect!" Elliot's comment made me feel even more satisfied.

"Now blow out the flame," Chester said as I lit the final candle.

I did as he instructed, then placed the burnt match a bit off to the side.

"Thank you," I said with a smile.

Chester nodded. "Of course." Then with a playful tone and a wink he added, "You've been doing well. Guess we'll keep ya around."

"I hate to admit the same, but he *has* been doing well." I glanced over my shoulder to surprisingly find Max. I hadn't heard him coming.

Is this really the same boy who seems to accuse me every chance he gets? Yet his tone and smile seemed genuine.

I cast my gaze down, not too sure how to react. "Thank you both. It really means a lot." I certainly wanted the group to think highly of me and wanted to fit in, but I didn't expect it to happen so suddenly.

Before either of them could respond, Annie and Jennifer raced to Max. "We're done!" They exclaimed, tugging on his arms. "Max, come play with us!"

Max grunted, rolling his eyes. "Oh, alright!" He pulled his arms gently from their grip. "Let me grab something first." I watched as he scooped up the Bibles into his arms before following the twins down the hall. I heard muffled creaks from the stairs as their voices grew faint.

Elliot came to my side as their voices faded, carefully picking up each candle and placing them individually into the muffin pan's cups. "Finally," he mumbled. "Some peace and quiet." His voice was heavy with sarcasm.

Carlotta bopped the back of his head playfully. "They only annoy us so much because they love us!"

Elliot smirked. "Whatever makes you and Max feel better about them following you two around like lost puppies. Once they're bored with him, they'll come bother you again."

Chester just shook his head as the two continued to banter. He gathered the tools into his arms before leaving the kitchen. I watched as he left, still unsure of exactly how old he was. He appeared much wiser and more mature than the others, and also kept mostly to himself. *Maybe he's in his twenties?* I wondered. It sure seemed likely.

"So, did you all make it to the abandoned church?" Carlotta's question drove through my thoughts. "And how was the farm? How's Ms. Martha doing?"

"We sure did," I answered, shifting my gaze back to the kitchen. Elliot was carefully placing the pots of water on top of the muffin pan, which now looked like a mini stove with the lit candles in it. "And Ms. Martha seems great! She and the other farmers were so kind and even had sandwiches for us."

Elliot perked up as he turned to face us after setting down the pots. "It was really good! You could definitely taste just how fresh the sandwiches were."

"Sounds like a fun trip!" Carlotta remarked, picking up her knitting tools. "I sure do miss Ms. Martha and her stories."

"Stories?" I asked.

Carlotta nodded as she started to knit. "Ms. Martha is full of stories. She traveled the world in her youth, lived and worked in other places before settling down here before the war. She got to see a lot of the world before it was destroyed."

"Really?" I'd never given much thought to how many adults had likely seen the world before it was destroyed by war. *They don't even realize how lucky they are!* I imagined other cities and great plains crowded with buffalo and towering mountains covered in snow, sights I'd only seen in old photographs. *I wish I could travel to other places!*

"Uh huh. I believe she even visited Jerusalem. You'll have to ask her about that," Carlotta said as Elliot checked the water for any signs of bubbles.

I straightened up at the mention of the Holy Land. As the three of us continued to chat while waiting for the water to boil, I felt even more intrigued by the farmer. I already knew without a doubt I would talk more with her my next trip to the farm.

Chapter Twenty-Three

"You're getting seconds?" Elliot asked as Kailey climbed to her feet. A smile lit his face. "It's that good?"

Kailey nodded. "It's lovely! Gotta fill up on good food whenever you've got the chance. After all, tomorrow isn't guaranteed!"

I bit into a carrot as she made her way over to the pots and sliced vegetables, scooping a bit more onto her plate. My meal of colorful vegetables, mashed potatoes, and eggs had been wonderful. I felt a sense of pride I'd helped contribute to this dinner.

My eyes trailed to where Max disappeared into the hallway, dressed as if heading somewhere.

"You know," Elliot nudged me, following my gaze. "You're free to come and go, too. Carlotta just asks that you're back before nightfall if possible. And let someone know where you're going. That way we can search for ya if you don't show back up."

I swallowed a mouthful of food, turning to meet his gaze as a thought popped into my mind. "Did you all send someone when Olivia and I didn't return?"

"Chester and I searched for you," Kailey answered, retaking her place at the table across from us. The rest of the group had already finished and gone downstairs. "Didn't know what happened to you two."

"We assumed you two wanted to be alone again, so we eventually stopped looking," Elliot added.

I sat back in my chair, fidgeting with some of my curls. *They really did all that for us?* I imagined them searching through the alleyways, calling for us but having to eventually give up as the night went on. I cast my gaze down as Kailey continued.

"Then I ran into you when I wasn't even looking," she said before biting into a potato.

I re-met her gaze. "I truly wanted to find my way back, but I couldn't figure it out," I stammered out between bites. *Why didn't I try harder to find them? Why did I give up so easily?* My shoulders dropped and I cast my gaze back down.

Elliot cleared his throat. "We understand," he said, giving me a quick pat on the shoulder which instantly caused me to feel less guilt. "We are pretty well hidden – which is good for our sake but bad for newbies. It would be hard for a stranger to find us. Heck, took me a while to figure out all these streets. They all look the same!"

I chuckled while Kailey nodded her head. "Yes," she said between bites. "I swear some streets are *identical*."

"Some of the houses are literally just different in color but everything else is the same," I quickly chimed in, thankful for the conversation change. I felt gratitude spread through me as I thought more about them searching for my sister and me. *They really care about me!*

"Have you seen the apartment complexes near Center City?" Elliot spoke up. "Now *those* are identical. And ugly, too."

Kailey giggled. "Tell me about it. I don't get how the city folks live in such ugly buildings. I couldn't do it."

As the three of us continued to munch and chat away, I felt an object hit the side of my foot. Leaning down, I picked up a small green marble and showed it to Kailey and Elliot.

"Looks like we've got company," Elliot smirked, turned in his chair to face the dark hallway as the twins emerged from it, both of them laughing uncontrollably.

"You should have seen your face!" Jennifer said between laughs. "You looked so confused, Oliver!"

"I was," I muttered, managing a laugh. I felt my face turning red after being singled out. *I guess it's to be expected as the newcomer*, I thought, my face cooling down as I realized they meant it playfully.

"What are you two up to now?" Kailey asked as they came to our side.

The twins exchanged a glance, their laughter slowly dying down. This time Annie spoke up.

"We want dessert! We demand cookies!"

Elliot slowly rose to his feet. "Ask nicely. What's the magic word?"

"Please!" The two girls said simultaneously.

"There it is," Elliot said, opening a top cabinet and reaching up to take out a blue bag. The twins jumped up and down as he did so. "Just a few each. You all don't need sugar."

The twins gleamed as they grabbed the cookies, thanking Elliot before bounding down the hall again.

"You keep food stored way up there?" I asked, watching as Elliot reached as high as he could to put the bag of cookies away. It seemed odd to keep food stashed so far out of reach.

"If we don't, they'll eat the entire bag," Kailey explained as Elliot returned to his seat next to me. "Those two would clear out all the junk food in a day if they could."

"We found that out the hard way," Elliot chuckled.

"You aren't hiding anything else in those tops shelves, are you?" I asked. Most of the lower shelves contained food along with cookware and utensils, while the old refrigerator in the kitchen corner was stocked with coolers to keep leftovers cool and produce fresh.

"Nothing interesting," Elliot remarked as he finished up his food. "Now, are you two going to finish eating anytime soon? I'd love to join the game downstairs sometime." His tone was playful, but I could sense a hint of urgency. The group played a variety of games in the evening together, something everyone looked forward to. It sucked missing out on them.

"My bad for getting seconds," Kailey laughed.

"We'll wait, just don't take too much longer!" Elliot said with a smile as I finished up my plate.

The three of us continued to chat away before heading downstairs. I eagerly followed my companions to the bean bag area where the rest of the group was engaged in a game with colorful cards. As I settled down among them, I felt joy spread through me to be part of a group I now knew cared so deeply about my well-being.

Chapter Twenty-Four

I shifted under my sheets, wrapping them tightly around me. About two weeks had passed since I rejoined the group. Each day was a new adventure of preparing meals, learning about my companions, playing games, and studying the Bible with Max. Our time reading and discussing ideas had caused the boy to warm up even more to me, and I was thankful for the thought-provoking insights he shared. He was full of knowledge but also fun to be around, something I never would have expected from our first encounter. It seemed like he had finally let go of the accusations and accepted my status as a member of the group.

I stared into the darkness, my eyes refusing to stay closed. Elliot was curled up in his corner, his laptop half open beside him. All but his legs were covered by the large sheet. I found out quickly that he truly did kick and move a lot in his sleep, leading me to move to the complete opposite side of the room to avoid injuries.

Yawning, I sat up and glanced around. Other than some moonlight filtering in from the kitchen windows, it was pitch black. I climbed to my feet, quietly entering the kitchen.

I was careful to take soft steps toward the sink. I did not want to wake Elliot or anyone downstairs. I turned the faucet on low and took a few sips before shutting it off. As I straightened back up, creaks from down the hall reached my ears.

Carefully and quietly, I peeked around the kitchen corner into the dark space.

"You up too?"

Carlotta stepped out of the darkness into the moonlight. Her green shirt hung off her tiny frame and her pink checkered pants dragged along the ground. A messy bun sat securely on top of her head, a few strands dangling free. She clutched her newest knitting project close to her chest, the rainbow yarn and needles sticking out as she came to my side. She touched her hearing aid briefly as she came closer.

"I'm just not tired," I responded.

She was quiet for a bit, her brows furrowing slightly. I watched her closely, speculating what could be on her mind.

"Well," she finally said, "I guess you can tag along. Otherwise, you'll forever wonder where I went."

"You're going somewhere?"

She just giggled, then motioned for me to follow as she turned down the hall. "Come on! There's something I'd like for you to see."

"Wait!" I sprinted to catch up as she disappeared down the hall. "But it's late and the others are sleeping, and—"

"Exactly! It's the perfect time to sneak away. Now be quiet and follow me!"

I trailed behind her through the darkness, not saying another word. *Why is she up so late? And why is she being so secretive?*

She led the way down the stairs and through the basement, pausing at the back door so we could put on our shoes. As we stepped into the breezy night air, I came to my companion's side. The bright full moon illuminated our path as we walked down the street.

"I want to show you something," Carlotta said as we reached the end of our street. "I like visiting alone at night. It's hard to leave during the day when everyone needs something or wants something."

I remained quiet as her words sunk in. It began to hit me why she had secretly snuck out — it was the only way for her to get some alone time. She rarely seemed to have a moment to herself. The twins hung around her like glue, and the other members of the group constantly needed something from her or had questions for her. I felt my shoulders drop. Being a leader didn't seem easy.

"Is it far?" was all I could manage to get out.

"Not too far. And trust me, it'll be worth it."

I didn't ask any more questions as we moved through the abandoned neighborhood. Although I had walked these streets for a while now, I still found the area confusing with all the twists and turns. The homes highly resembled one another with their decay and overgrown, weed-infested yards. I couldn't imagine navigating the area solo.

We eventually exited the neighborhood into some trees. Other than vegetation creeping up their trunks, the trees here were bare. Way more bare than other woods and the forest.

The trees grew thicker and closer together the farther we walked. Crickets chirped in the distance and an owl hoot came from deeper in the woods. I pushed through the heavy weeds, eager to keep up with Carlotta as the trees and darkness seemed to close in on us.

"I know this may seem a bit scary, but I promise we're almost there!" she said as if reading my thoughts.

"We better be!"

Thankfully, Carlotta's words proved true as the trees thinned out. We emerged into a small clearing roughly about the size of our house. The moonlight shone down to reveal a small pond up ahead. Lily pads and pink flowers covered the stagnant surface. To the right of the pond stood an old red truck. Its doors were missing and weeds poked through the seats and the tires, one of which was also missing.

"I like to come here." Carlotta took some steps toward the pond. "It's the perfect place to get away from the world and the pressure that comes with being leader." She sat down at the pond's edge and started to knit. "Here, it feels like everything is okay. I can just *be*, I can just exist for a minute."

I sat down beside her, not wanting to make eye contact. Although her words were gentle and she seemed unbothered by my presence, I couldn't help feeling guilty over pestering her with so many questions since rejoining the group. The last thing I wanted was to further burden her or add more stress.

"It sure is pretty," I said as I gazed at the pond. My eyes rested on one of the pink flowers. Its petals stretched out across the surrounding lily pads. As I focused on it more, a memory came rushing back of my sister wearing a similar flower pin in her hair throughout our childhood. Picturing Olivia smiling as we played together in the memory caused me to blink my eyes quickly to stop the tears.

"Oliver?" Carlotta's voice drove away my thoughts. "Are you alright?"

"Sorry," I gulped. I did not want to ruin her moment of peace, and I wanted to appear strong. "I just miss her at times." I didn't specify who, but I knew she'd know. News spread quickly through the group.

Carlotta was silent for a moment before speaking again. "Do you need a moment?"

I shook my head, hoping I could shake away the memories. I did my best to hold back the tears, but to no avail. I turned away as they rushed down my cheeks.

"I'm sorry," I muttered softly. "I just don't want to be weak right now." *I wish I had Olivia's barrette!* Having it on me and squeezing it gave me comfort. But alas, it was back with my belongings at the house, and I was here.

"You know," Carlotta shifted closer to me, continuing to knit as she spoke. "It's not weak to cry, or show emotion. Your tears are all the love you had for Olivia. They're a symbol of how much you loved her and there's nothing weak about that." She paused as I sniffled. "Oliver, I know your faith is important to you, and the Scriptures tell us that even Jesus cried. He cried out of His love for Lazarus and the people. And I don't think anyone would *ever* consider Jesus weak."

I sniffled again, wiping my eyes. Her words struck me as I recalled the Gospel passage from John. I realized I could not debunk her words. She was right, Jesus *did* cry at the death of Lazarus. Jesus cried despite knowing Lazarus would live again. People watched Jesus weep, and no one called Him weak. Jesus was strong, the strongest there ever was! I straightened up, feeling a bit better as I reflected on Carlotta's words. *If Christ's tears didn't make Him weak, then maybe my tears don't make me weak, either. I can cry, and also be strong too,* I thought to myself. *Maybe it's okay to feel what I need to feel.*

"You're so good at this," I said between tears, turning back to her. "You always seem to know the right words!"

Carlotta chuckled, blushing slightly. "Well, I'm no stranger to grief. I had to think a lot about death, and faith, and what all I believe in after I lost someone close to me."

"What happened? Who did you lose?"

Carlotta drew in a deep breath before speaking again. "Jordyn was like a sister to me. We escaped from a regulator station together and were inseparable after that. She knew everything about me, and I knew everything about her. She understood me like no other." She paused briefly. "We founded the group together a few years back. We wanted to create a safe space for teens like us, teens with nowhere else to go.

She was actually my second in command before she passed." I watched her intently as she stared into the pond. I could tell this was a painful memory for her.

"If it's too much, you don't have to share." I already knew what came next, but still wanted to give Carlotta the space to share if she wanted to. It was obvious just how important Jordyn was to her and just how painful this memory was.

She glanced up briefly, managing a small smile. "No, it's okay. Thank you, though." She cast her gaze back down. "It all happened shortly after we decided to join the Uprising. Jordyn was beyond excited to participate in our first attack. It seemed like we had the upper hand at first, but things quickly turned for the worse. The Uprising was a lot smaller back then and as I noticed new regulators arriving on the scene, I ordered my crew to pull back." She gulped. "The regulators were fast, and they didn't hesitate to start aiming at us. Some of the bullets hit Jordyn and s-she just . . . collapsed. We tried carrying her back home, but it was too late. She lost too much blood, and we weren't able to save her." She stopped, pressing her lips together and closing her eyes tightly. She paused from knitting. Slowly, she took a few breaths then rose to her feet, tucking her knitting supplies under her arm.

"It took months for me to realize it wasn't my fault," Carlotta said as I also stirred to my feet. I followed as we strolled around the truck to the other side of the pond. I felt a knot in my stomach once I noticed a small stone and the uneven ground. The two of us came to a stop at the edge of the grave.

"We decided to bury her here. It's another reason I like this place." She glanced at me briefly before whispering, "I know it may sound a bit strange, but I often feel like she's still here when I visit. I feel so much peace at this pond."

"It doesn't sound strange at all," I reassured her, my eyes locked on the gray stone that had the name 'Jordyn' scratched into it. I expected Carlotta to say more, but she remained silent as she stood over her friend's grave. I glanced around us, the trees dark and looming and the pond glowing under the moonlight. A bubble broke the surface of the pond, and I wondered what might be lurking below the lily pads.

"You've been very strong," I finally broke the silence. "I know Jordyn would be proud of you and how well you manage the group. You're a brilliant leader."

Carlotta smiled. "One of the last things she told me was how proud she was of the leader I had become. It isn't easy, especially knowing the same fate may await any of you. But I want to stay strong and be more careful so as to not lose anyone else." She turned to meet my gaze. "People like Jordyn and Olivia are worth fighting for, but know they're just as proud of us when we stay behind to protect our home." She looked back over her friend's grave. "I hope you know, Oliver, that Olivia would be proud of your strength as well."

"Thank you." I didn't feel strong at all, but I wasn't about to let Carlotta know that. Breathing in deeply, I asked, "How long did it take, for the grief to leave?"

Carlotta was quiet for a bit. "I don't have an answer to that, because it hasn't left. But I will tell you, it gets easier with time. Easier to talk about, easier to remember. You don't feel like breaking down into tears every time." She straightened up a bit. "I like to imagine grief as a heavy backpack. At first you can't believe how heavy it is, and you have no clue how you'll be able to carry it. But over time, you get used to how heavy it is and start to carry it with ease. You grow stronger and get better, but that doesn't mean the backpack suddenly becomes light. It's still just as heavy but you've grown into someone who can handle the weight, someone who can carry it." She turned to meet my gaze. "And you will grow into someone who can carry this in time. I promise."

I cast my gaze downward, letting her words sink in. Olivia's death felt like the heaviest backpack of all, much heavier than any backpack before. I was slowly learning how to carry it, but my shoulders ached. I could only hope my leader's words would come true in time.

The two of us remained in silence for a bit longer, glancing down at the earth that now held Jordyn's body. I thought about where I had buried Olivia. *How do their graves look now?* I wondered. *Oh, I really hope the crosses are still standing and the regulators didn't go over there and mess things up!* Shaking away the worry, I bowed my head to pray silently.

"Well," Carlotta said after a few minutes. "We better be heading back so we can get some rest. I'm ready whenever you are, but no rush."

I nodded, looking once more over Jordyn's grave before meeting Carlotta's eyes. "Lead the way."

And with that, the two of us entered the dark trees once again.

Chapter Twenty-Five

I strolled into the kitchen, my belly full and my spirits high. Carlotta glanced up as I did so, pausing from her task to greet me. Small containers were spread out on the counter before her, all stuffed to the brim with a mysterious mixture I assumed was from our lunch leftovers. I counted ten of them.

"Do you need any help?" I asked, coming to her side. We had grown closer since our walk to the pond a few nights ago. I enjoyed helping her with tasks around the house, which seemed to be never-ending. She and Chester were always cleaning or patching things up. I just hoped I was able to alleviate their stress in some way.

"Well actually," she said, wiping her hands on a nearby towel. "If you'd like to join Trevor and me on our cat run, we'd appreciate the help carrying all these."

"A *cat run?* What's that?"

She smiled. "Trevor and I like to go feed the stray cats, and spend some time with them. We nicknamed it a cat run, but really, it's just us taking care of the strays in the area. It's actually what we were up to when we first met you." Softening her voice, she added, "It really helps Trevor relax and feel more grounded. Maybe it could help you in your grief?"

I nodded. *So that's why so many cats linger in the area.* "I'd love to!"

She grinned, grabbing an old bucket. "You want to be in charge of carrying this?" She asked, beginning to fill the bucket with the small containers. "And don't worry, you'll get plenty of time petting them, too."

"Sounds great!" I said, helping her fill up the bucket. After all the containers were securely placed, we exited the kitchen and descended the stairs. The bucket was heavier than I expected, but not so heavy it weighed me down. I clutched it close to my chest once I realized the handle was broken.

"Trevor!" Carlotta called, knocking on his door. "It's time for a cat run!"

The boy emerged from his room within seconds. He wore all black, including his durag.

"It feels like our last one was forever ago!" He raised an eyebrow as he noticed me carrying the bucket. "Oliver, are you coming, too?"

"Sure am!"

The boy smiled. "Great! I can introduce you to all of them. I've named them *all*."

"He sure has!" Carlotta said with a smile, leading us toward the back door. We waved at the rest of the group as we passed them. They sat on the bean bag chairs in a circle as if in discussion.

I shrank back a bit as we stepped out of the basement into the hot day. It remained bitterly hot even as the days passed. Thankfully, I had a good reason to leave the cool house and venture out into the unpleasant weather.

"Unfortunately, we do have to walk for a bit," Carlotta told me as we crossed the backyard. "We can't place the food anywhere too close or it might draw regulators. They follow the cats sometimes and have stolen a few."

"What do they do with them?" I asked, thinking back to the stray the regulators had caught the first time Olivia and I explored the old yellow house.

"We're not sure," Carlotta said, guiding us through the abandoned streets. "We just hope it's nothing bad."

I nodded. "I hope the same."

The three of us continued, Trevor taking the lead at points. We traveled deep into the abandoned neighborhood, taking plenty of twists and turns. I moved the bucket to my other hand, leaning it up against my hip as we walked on.

"There's some up here!" Trevor called, bounding up a crumbling driveway to an old gray house. A few cats rushed to meet him, rubbing against his legs.

Carlotta reached into the bucket. "Oliver, let's place a few here. It seems to be a popular spot today!"

I nodded, crouching down to place some of the small containers next to the one Carlotta laid down. The cats rushed over as we did so, rubbing against us. I reached out, petting a skinny gray cat that rubbed against me before diving into the food.

"They're so soft!" I exclaimed. I had never actually touched one before. "And so cute!"

"Aren't they?" Trevor smiled, coming to our side. "That gray one is named Millie," he pointed to the one I had petted. "The smaller tabby is Shelby, and the bigger one is Shadow. The orange one is Spike."

"I love them all already!" I said, watching proudly as they chewed away.

"Yes, they're a lovely bunch!" Carlotta said. "But we need to keep going. There's more to feed, and they don't like to be bothered during their mealtime."

"Where can we find more?" I asked as we turned to leave, readjusting the bucket against my hip.

"They'll start emerging as we continue," Trevor answered, coming to my side as we exited the driveway. "There's a few more that linger around this area."

Sure enough, more cats slowly but surely emerged. All the cats were friendly and I was happy to pet them all. A few even climbed onto Trevor's lap, giving the boy lots of face rubs. Eventually, my bucket became empty as our smiles became full.

"Well, that's all the food!" I said, petting a calico that rubbed against my legs. I sat down, allowing the cat to climb into my lap as I continued to pet it. I sat the bucket down beside me.

Almost as soon as I got comfortable, a siren cut through the air. I jumped to my feet as my companions did the same. A few of the cats dashed behind the nearest house while others continued eating, completely unfazed by the noise.

"Quick!" Carlotta said, heading toward the house. "We can hide in here!"

The three of us ran into the house, staying close to one another as we ascended stairs to a small vacant room. Carlotta instantly shut and locked the door behind us.

"Oh no!" I mumbled as I crouched down. "I left the bucket outside! The regulators will see it!"

"It's fine," Carlotta whispered. "The containers are out there too. If they take them, oh well. We have others back home."

I nodded, my eyes slowly focusing in the dark room. I watched as Trevor crawled toward a window and peeked out.

"Anyone out there?" Carlotta asked, coming to his side. As the two of them looked out, my mind drifted back to the yellow house and Olivia's certainty that she saw someone in one of the house's windows.

Perhaps you did see someone, Olivia. I thought about the locked doors. *Was anyone hiding behind them?* My thoughts of that day and then my sister started to consume me, and soon a few tears rolled down my cheeks. I didn't even care to hide them.

"Oliver, this regulator looks like you!" Trevor's statement cut through my thoughts, bringing me back to the present. Wiping my tears, I slowly approached the window the two barely peeked through, just enough to see out into the street below.

"They're not coming in here, are they?" I asked as I got closer.

"Nope! They're getting back in their car," Carlotta reassured me as I glanced out for myself.

What I saw startled me to my core. Climbing into the passenger seat was a boy presumably around my age with blue eyes and dirty blond hair that curled exactly like mine. He too had a slender frame, and his facial features were similar to my own. I watched intently as he sat down into the seat and closed the door. Even the way he moved felt familiar. It was like looking into a mirror.

I pulled myself away from the window, leaning back against the wall for support. My heart pounded in my chest. *Why do I look like a regulator? Or rather, why does he look like me?* A regulator was the last thing I wanted to resemble. The memory of the regulator sent shivers down my spine as I slowly sat on the ground.

"You don't happen to be related to one of them, do you?" Trevor asked, sitting next to me. "Did you come from a regulator family, by chance? Or were you with the city folk before joining us?" Although his words felt accusatory, I knew he meant nothing malicious by them. His voice was full of concern.

I shook my head as Carlotta sat in front of me. "He's not, Trevor." Her voice was firm but gentle. "Oliver has a pretty generic look for a white boy. I'm sure it's just a strange coincidence."

Carlotta's words soothed me, but I still felt deeply disturbed. "Yeah, I'm sure that's the case." I couldn't imagine otherwise. "Since they've left now, can we please leave?"

"Of course," Carlotta said, rising to her feet. "Trevor, do you mind carrying the bucket home and picking up the empty containers on the way back? I think Oliver might like some time to think."

"I can certainly do that!" Trevor responded as we climbed to our feet.

I remained silent as I followed the two of them out the room and out the house. I mainly stayed to myself as we made the journey back home, trailing a bit behind my companions as the image of the regulator flashed through my mind. *Who was he, and why did he look nearly identical to me? Would I ever come across him again, and if I did, would our similar looks make him hesitant to hurt me?* I shook my mind clear as the basement I had come to know so well came into view. All I knew for certain was that it was good to be back home.

Chapter Twenty-Six

I stirred on my bean bag chair, getting up to stretch. I had ventured downstairs to read while the rest of the group finished up their breakfast. My breakfast of mixed cereal and toast hit the spot despite being slightly stale. Meals here were wonderful, and I felt a sense of pride that I had been able to contribute to the food pile and meal prepping in recent weeks.

I walked along the shelves, eventually picking up one of the Bibles we had brought back from the abandoned church. Leaning against the shelves, I flipped through the pages. As I did so, I thought back to the strange occurrence the other day. I had confided in Elliot and Max about the regulator, but none of us could come up with any explanation that satisfied me. I was okay with looking like city folks, but the thought of resembling a regulator disgusted me. Shaking the feeling away, I focused on the Bible passage I had flipped to.

I paused as I glanced over the page. Someone had written notes in the margins. From the doodles that were also scattered about, I guessed it must've been Sid, who was upstairs now with the others.

A creak from the stairs caused me to glance up. Kailey gently stepped off the stairs, a cup in hand. On top the cup was a scrap of paper, which she held in place securely with her other hand.

"What kind of bug is it this time?" I asked as she crossed the basement, her back straight and her head held high.

"A sweet little caterpillar!" she called out, not breaking her stride. "I can't blame the poor thing for coming inside. I'd do the same to get away from the heat!"

I watched as she opened the door. "I'd do the same, too."

Kailey propped open the door to release the bug. "Now if only we could get the others to understand!" As soon as a small green critter crawled out, she closed the door. "Back to the heat he goes!"

I chuckled as she crossed the basement and ascended the stairs. With a smile, I glanced back down at the Bible.

My gaze paused as I read over the notes written in the white space of 3 John. Scribbled in the space were bullet points about showing hospitality and taking care of strangers, with links to Bible verses such as Leviticus 19:34, Matthew 25:35, and Hebrews 13:2.

"Even if someone is a stranger to us," I whispered the final bullet point out loud. "They are someone who is beloved by God." Flipping back a bit, I landed on another marked-up page in the Book of Acts. "There will always be people who mock and don't support you," I whispered the note next to Acts 2:13 out loud. "Don't let that stop you from spreading the Good News of Christ Jesus." I glanced at the words scribbled alongside verse thirty. "God keeps His words/promises." I flipped ahead a few chapters, passing notes about Jesus's Lordship and more doodles. I paused as I reached the book of Romans, a book that always troubled me. Sid had marked many verses throughout the first chapter.

As I read over some of her notes, footsteps came bounding down the stairs. I turned, shutting the Bible slowly as Jennifer and Annie raced toward me. The two were inseparable.

"Oliver! You're going to the Uprising meeting tonight? Max said you were," Jennifer questioned as the twins came to a halt before me, their faces lit with smiles and wide eyes.

"Oh!" I chuckled. "I've been thinking about it. I think it's time I attend one." I cast my gaze back to the stairs as Max came rushing down, Kailey close behind him. The two had confirmed their attendance already.

The twins turned to face them as they joined us. "Oliver said he's still thinking about it," Jennifer announced before anyone could say anything. I held back a laugh as Max rolled his eyes.

"Great," Max muttered. "Yapper one and yapper two! Lucky me."

"Hey!" Kailey nudged him, a smile on her face. "You yap just as much, if not more!"

I giggled. "And I don't even yap that much!"

Max laughed. "We'll see about that tonight." He took on a more serious tone. "Anyways, word slipped out. But it's still your choice, Oliver. You don't have to go if you don't want to, but we'd enjoy the company." His tone was surprisingly gentle.

All eyes turned to me as I thought it over. A few others bounded down the stairs. Not wanting to have more eyes on me, I quickly made my decision. "I'm going."

Annie and Jennifer gave an excited squeal before heading toward the corner bean bag chairs. Max and Kailey looked pleased with my answer.

"Awesome," Max said. "We'll come get you when it's time."

"Make sure you eat a bit more before heading out. Meetings can get long, and it is a bit of a hike there," Kailey added before heading toward Carlotta.

I nodded, still glancing over those who had come downstairs. Max gave me a nod before heading toward the bean bag he'd been reading on this morning, his book wide open on top the chair. As I realized Sid was not among those who came downstairs, I clutched the Bible close to my chest and headed upstairs.

I found her in the kitchen, finishing up her food alone at the table. She took a bite out of an apple as I took a seat across from her.

"I noticed your notes and doodles." I smiled, setting the Bible on the table. "They're really insightful."

She swallowed before speaking. "Thank you. It's really just . . . whatever comes to mind as I'm reading." She glanced away, laughing slightly. "I think I've marked up nearly half the books down there with my doodles."

I smiled even wider. "No, I think it's really cool!" I leaned in. "If you don't mind me asking, how long have you believed?" As I glanced over her bracelets, I noticed a rainbow W.W.J.D. bracelet tied across her left wrist. I hadn't realized she also had faith. I had been under the impression that Max and I were the only believers among the group.

"Hmm, I'd say only about half my life? Since I could really understand the theology, you know?" She finished up her apple after she answered.

I nodded, opening the Bible and flipping through it. "You seem to really get it, I mean, you've marked up most of it!"

She chuckled, smiling slightly. "The Holy Spirit really helps me; I like to pray for the Spirit's guidance before reading. And I did have a Bible before joining the group, way back when I was living underground. So, it's not like I'm new to it all." She gently pushed her empty plate to the side so she could better see the Bible. I turned it sideways so we could both see.

"You understand Romans?" I asked as I flipped to the first chapter of the biblical book. "Paul seems so harsh at times. I know there's a few different interpretations over the ending of the first chapter."

I thought back to the heated debates that would sometimes occur among those at the orphanage. Those frustrating conversations instilled a fear in me that still lingered heavily. "I know about the first Corinthians mistranslation, well most people do, and it's pretty obvious Sodom and Gomorrah deals with inhospitality and attempted sexual violence, but I'm still stuck on this one when it comes to understanding same-sex relations." I lowered my voice slightly, not sure who was within earshot. Elliot's space was right around the corner and not everyone had gone downstairs. "You see, I don't experience attraction often, like rarely ever! But I have a little bit toward the same gender. So, understanding this passage is pretty important to me."

Sid nodded; her eyes soft. "I understand. I mean," she paused, glancing away and blushing slightly. "I'm a lesbian, so I've had to dig into those passages as well." She leaned closer to the open Bible. "How familiar are you with the start of Romans?"

I felt myself relax as her words sunk in. I had never opened up about my sexuality before, but I felt God telling me it was okay and that I was safe. I glanced over the words in Romans. "I'd say fairly familiar. I really struggle with chapter one, especially verses twenty-six through twenty-seven, plus the end of that passage. I don't feel like all those words starting in verse twenty-nine accurately describe me, and it's just . . . hard. Makes me not want to read the rest of Romans."

Sid nodded, beginning to point to the verses. "I get it. So, basically, that whole narrative starts in verse eighteen. Paul starts talking about the ancient pagans who lived alongside those early Christians. Like here." She pointed to verses twenty-one through twenty-three. "The people described in these verses are outsiders—*pagans*—who worshipped animals and creation instead of God. The text also repeats this in verse twenty-five." She moved her finger to that verse.

"Okay," I said, reading along.

"So, this all indicates Paul is writing with a *particular* group of people in mind, that is, the ancient Roman pagans who lived alongside the early Roman Christians. His audience, those Christians, would have known these pagans and been familiar with them. They probably had a certain view of these pagans, like the stereotypes Paul listed in verses twenty-nine through thirty-two.

"Paul sets this up in a way to trap his audience and expose their biases toward the pagans. That's why chapter two starts the way it does. He's reminding his audience they have no right to judge the pagans because we are all sinners in need of God's grace. The text also seems to indicate the early believers did some of the same things they hated the pagans for, like at the end of the first verse in chapter two, where Paul says, 'because you who pass judgement do the same things.'" She traced along the bottom of the verse as she read it out loud. "They were being hypocrites and judgmental toward the pagans."

"Alright." My eyes glanced over the words. "Paul's writing about pagans. I get that but I'm still a bit confused. Didn't those pagans engage in same-sex acts? And doesn't the text say that's wrong?"

Sid shook her head. "Yes, but no. It's important to remember the *context* in which those acts occurred. What Paul described here was pagan idolatry, not innate sexual orientation. And when idol worship happens in the Bible, what often accompanies it is sex acts and orgies. I'm sure you're familiar with the golden calf in Exodus." When I nodded, she continued, "The people worshipped the golden calf, then had an orgy. Paul affirms this in his first letter to the Corinthians, chapter ten verses seven and eight." She paused. "That doesn't make sex in totality bad, just condemns it when done to worship idols. Likewise, the acts in this Romans passage were done in the context of idol worship. They were simply that; sex done as part of idol worship rituals."

"Okay," I muttered. "So, you believe Paul's just describing sex acts here, not relationships? And that sex took place as part of pagan worship rituals or even orgies?"

"Yes, precisely. Another important thing I noticed is the text says '*their* women' meaning these women were already with the pagan men. They were in heterosexual relationships and were not homosexuals. These were straight pagans, in straight relationships, who engaged in acts outside their marriages as part of idol worship."

"That means they cheated on their spouse!"

Sid smiled. "Yep! Interesting how that gets left out of the conversation, isn't it? So, these pagans went against their partner to engage in sex acts that would have felt unnatural to *them* because they were not attracted to those of the same sex. What's happening here is a lot different than what me and you feel, isn't it?"

I nodded. "Then the usage of unnatural in the verses refers to what felt unnatural to them, right?"

"That's a possible interpretation. It's also likely it referred to something considered unnatural during the time period in which Paul wrote it. If you haven't noticed, the text never actually *says* women engaged sexually with other women. It just says they did something unnatural, which meant a lot of different things back when Paul was writing this letter. If the women dominated, for example, the sex would be considered unnatural, even if with a man. Most oral and anal intercourse were also considered unnatural during that time and culture, even when done by a heterosexual couple." She leaned back in her chair. "There's actually some historical evidence both the men and women in this passage engaged with male priests at pagan places of worship."

"Really?" I perked up. "Where did you learn that?"

"There's a book downstairs that goes over it in depth. It also explains other Bible passages often believed to condemn same-sex couples. It has a pretty cover of a Bible with flowers stemming from it. I'd highly recommend it."

"I'll have to check that out!" I leaned back myself, feeling more relaxed and like I grasped her interpretation. "So, the Romans passage, it's not condemning same-sex couples? But condemns sex done in the context of idol worship?"

"Right. It's about pagans engaging sexually with one another as part of their idolatry. The text doesn't describe same-sex couples, nor does it even discuss sexual orientation. Those verses depict sex done as part of idol worship, not homosexuals in loving and committed relationships."

"That must be why verse twenty-six starts with 'because of this.' It's because of their idol worship they engaged in those acts."

"Yep! It's a lot different from how you and I feel."

I smiled, closing the Bible and pulling it close to me. "Thank you so much for this, Sid. It really helps. Are you heading downstairs by chance?" I was hoping she could show me the book she suggested.

She shook her head, slowly getting up. I also got up, making sure to tuck the chair in as I secured the Bible in my arms. "Nah," she said, tossing the rest of the apple in the trash bin and placing her plate in the sink. "I think I'm going to bother Elliot for a bit." She glanced back at me. "But you take care, Oliver, and know I'm always up for a Bible discussion. May God guide you and bring you the answers you seek."

"May God guide you, too!"

And with that, she disappeared into Elliot's room as I headed downstairs, eager to get my hands on that book and learn more.

Chapter Twenty-Seven

"Not much farther!" Dallas called from up ahead.

Harriet sighed, trailing a little bit behind her right-hand man. Her hands traced along the walls and their unique patterns and markings, patterns and markings she knew all too well. This tunnel had once connected to a government-run fallout shelter, just like the one she grew up in. Her thoughts had been heavy lately with memories of her parents. The last memory of them stirred within her as she traced along a symbol that was slowly fading.

She could still picture them in her mind, although their faces had gone blurry over the years. The last time she saw them, the three of them were at the entrance to a large ship. Harriet closed her eyes as the memory washed over her. She desperately wanted to remember as much of her parents as she could. From what she could recall, both of them were frail. Her mom had suffered great hair loss from the radiation and had an awful cough. Her dad also coughed and had some large skin rashes on his arms.

"You'll understand one day, once you're older," her father had said as the ship sounded its horn. "You'll be safer over there."

"And don't forget," her mother had added, kissing her forehead. "God is watching over you and will always take good care of you." Her parents had hugged her tightly that day before she was rushed into a ship with other children, given over by parents who looked just as rough. Harriet had forgotten much of the voyage, but the memory of being rushed off by guards into a spacious fallout shelter lingered vividly. The guards were brutal, as were the adults that taught the children who had come from all over the world.

She had *hated* her time in the shelter. The adults had been harsh, and fiercely loyal to the emperor. The leader had gained popularity and the trust of the people by establishing a safe, secure, and clean haven in a world wrecked by the horrors of nuclear war. He gave people a sense of hope in the first few years with his operations to clean up the environment, but was quick to indoctrinate the newer generations in the belief that it was also necessary to clean up the population as well, an operation that never sat well with Harriet's soul. Some truly believed, and others pledged their loyalty to the emperor out of fear of what might happen to them or family members if they refused. Plenty of former military and police evolved into regulators, along with many of the kids who were brought over with Harriet.

Nearly everything the adults taught had raised her suspicions, from the strict education, to having to wear blue contacts and constantly bleach her dark hair, to lessons about how the emperor was the "one true God" and only some were worthy of inheriting the life they would receive on the surface.

No part of her had wanted to return to the surface unless her parents were up there waiting for her. She had gotten in quite a lot of trouble too, for refusing to worship and bow down to pictures of the emperor, and her punishment got worse the older she grew and the louder she got. The adults in the shelter labeled her "stubborn" and "disobedient," labels she proudly wore now as part of the Uprising.

Her stubborn, rebellious nature had sparked an interest in some of the other children, many of whom shared the same concerns but quietly. One of those children was Dallas. The two of them started to meet and discuss the lessons they were being taught and work to debunk them. Eventually, some of the other children joined in, and the twelve of them set out on a mission to fight back and resist. Although their quiet nonviolent methods had failed to produce change, they brought more individuals into their movement. She never could have imagined back then how large the resistance would become, and she immediately felt a rush of gratitude as she thought about the recent growth the Uprising had experienced.

She lifted her hand off the wall, racing to catch up with her dearest friend. He turned to acknowledge her as she did so and the two began to walk side by side.

"They're such ugly symbols, aren't they?" Dallas nodded to the symbols she had just been tracing. "I can't stand what they represent."

"Me neither," Harriet responded as the two traveled through the tunnels. Although they were dark and stretched all under the city, the leader knew them like the back of her hand. There wasn't a single turn or twist that she wasn't familiar with.

"Can we please get some food after this meeting?"

Harriet snickered. "Did you not eat before?"

"Yes," Dallas grumbled. "But I'm still hungry."

"Of course we can. There's plenty of food back home," Harriet responded, thinking about their recently gathered harvest. Their small garden had produced a bountiful yield of various fruits and vegetables. She was looking forward to bringing some next time to distribute among the Uprising.

The two walked on in silence for a bit longer. The shelter holding the approaching meeting wasn't too far off now.

"Have you ever considered . . ." Dallas paused for a moment, running his hands through his hair. "Oh, I don't know! Maybe packing up, gathering our forces, and settling elsewhere? We have enough people to start our own city. I'm sure we could find pockets of people out there somewhere. It would sure beat having to fight and hide from regulators all the time."

"The rest of the world is either destroyed or contaminated," Harriet pointed out as the two turned a corner into a wider hallway. "Besides, we have every right to be here, just as much as the emperor and his regulators. This is our home now too. We can't just run away from that or from creating a better world for the next generation. They deserve to inherit so much better, and all the unworthies being born right now have a right to their life, don't you think?"

Dallas sighed. "Yeah, you're right." He nudged his companion playfully. "As usual."

Harriet smiled, not saying anything else as they rounded another corner. During these uncertain and scary times, she was thankful to have her childhood friend by her side. If her time in the government-run fallout shelter had brought anything good, it was their friendship.

Chapter Twenty-Eight

"It's right around the corner!" Kailey promised as we cut through an abandoned alleyway. I never could have guessed just how far the suburbs spread, and I was in awe of the many unique neighborhoods built from marble, brick, and colorful wood. Plenty of homes retained excellent form despite years of abandonment.

Kailey led Max and me up the stairs of an old marble building with tall columns and large windows. "We cut through here to get into the tunnels," Kailey said to me as we entered the dimly lit space. The setting sun cast rays through the building's windows.

"Tunnels?" The only tunnels I'd been in were those connecting together the bunkers back at the orphanage. Even then, those small tunnels had felt more like hallways.

"Yes," Max replied as he and Kailey removed their sunglasses. "We use the fallout tunnels to get to the Uprising. Many of them still reside underground." My companions moved deeper into the dark building.

I followed closely, barely able to see in the poorly lit space. The weak glow from Max's flashlight hardly helped my eyes adjust. I placed my hand over my pocket, feeling for Olivia's barrette. I wanted to bring her with me on my adventures, especially the one we were embarked on now. *Wish you were here, Liv*, I thought, blinking as my eyes adjusted to the dark building. She had been so excited at the thought of joining the Uprising. *If only the bullets had missed! She would be here now too . . .*

"The furniture back here is so dusty!" Kailey's statement cut through my thoughts. I raced after her toward an old wooden table. "I've been drawing on it," she said as I reached her side. Her fingers traced through the dust, making two dashes and a curved line beneath them. "It's a smiley face!"

I giggled. "I see it!" I drew my own among a table full of small doodles.

Max added a few doodles of his own before continuing down the hall. "Come on you two! We can't write in the dust all day!"

The three of us walked on through the darkness. *How big can one building be?* I wondered as we wandered from hall to hall. It seemed to have no end. *How did they figure this place out?*

"There's some stairs down here," Max told me when we turned down another dark hall. "Just be careful, and take your time. Grab the back of my shirt if you need."

"I definitely will!" I chuckled as I took hold of his shirt. As the three of us descended the stairs I clung tightly to Max, carefully moving my feet down one step at a time.

The sound of Kailey opening a large door ahead cut through the silence as Max and I leaped off the final step. I let go of his shirt as we came to her side. The space behind the door led to a large, curved hall with overhead lights. I was thankful to finally have some actual lighting after walking through the dark for so long.

I trailed behind my two friends into the cold gray tunnel. The walls were rough, with ragged edges and rocks that poked out here and there. Many of the lights flickered and a couple had burned out completely. Along some of the walls were unfamiliar symbols and other markings. I was amazed at how well they were preserved, and even more amazed at how my companions seemed to know exactly where to turn as the tunnel opened up to others.

"Is this how you always get to meetings?" I asked as we descended down some more steps into a narrower tunnel.

"Yep!" Kailey answered, still in the lead.

"I used to live down here before joining the group," Max said from a few steps ahead of me. "We'll run into some of my old comrades in just a moment."

His words made me shiver. I couldn't imagine living down here with the cold and stale air. The dampness and narrow tunnels felt so cramped. It wasn't nearly as colorful or bright as the orphanage's bunker, and nothing compared to living on the surface. I couldn't imagine ever living underground again now that I'd experienced the surface.

After a few more steps, the tunnel opened into a large room lit with flashlights and lanterns, similar to our home. Stacks of supplies stood around the space along with cot beds, many of which had people lounging or sitting on them. A few individuals came forward to meet us, instantly recognizing Kailey and Max.

"Everyone, this is Oliver, who's been staying with us for a while now," Max nodded toward me as they gathered around us.

"Good to meet you all!" I said, smiling meekly as multiple eyes scanned me.

As Max and Kailey conversed with those who lived here, movement out of the corner of my eye caught my attention. An individual slowly rose from his cot and began to walk toward us. I felt a smile spread across my lips as I recognized the boy's features in the dim lighting.

No, it can't be!

"Caleb!" I rushed to hug my friend as he got closer. *How on earth did he survive?* I pulled away, glancing over my childhood friend with the widest smile. His eyes were just as friendly as I remembered, although his clothes were a lot more ragged now and he had lost his tan.

"I thought that was you!" Caleb chuckled. "But I wasn't sure until they said your name."

"How . . . what?" I breathed out. I couldn't contain my smile. "How did you survive? I mean . . ." I broke off into laughter, hugging my friend once more.

"It wasn't easy, but I found the Uprising pretty quickly," he said, pulling away from the hug. "Or really, they found me." He nodded toward a few others as they approached us. Kailey and Max instantly flanked me on either side. "I had to get off the surface almost immediately, and they brought me down here. It's been a bit of an adjustment, livin' under again."

Before I could respond, Kailey stepped forward. "What's going on here?" Her eyes were locked on Caleb.

I turned to her, then to Max. "This is my friend Caleb. We lived together before I joined the group."

"Well, good to meet you then." Max shook his hand. "A friend of Oliver's is a friend of mine as well. Will you be joining the meeting?"

Caleb met my gaze once again. "I guess I am now." I felt a lightness in my chest as I met his gaze, my mouth still stretched in a smile.

"It would be wise to get going, like *now*." A tall individual spoke up. "The meeting is scheduled to start within a few minutes." As he glanced down at his watch, I realized just how little I paid attention to time since leaving the orphanage. Other than Max's old battery-powered alarm clock, those of us in the group rose with the sun and slept when it slept. We ate when we were hungry, and time had become irrelevant for the most part. But now it was necessary.

Max murmured something to the tall individual, and then those of us gathered continued on down the tunnels. Caleb came to my side as we left the large room and entered a narrow tunnel.

"Did any of the others survive?" I asked him, my thoughts racing at the possibility that others we had grown up with might be safe somewhere out there.

"Not sure," he admitted. "I ran off as soon as I could, and just kept goin'. Some of the regulators tried to pursue me, but they had no luck. That night, Catherine found me and brought me down here." He nodded toward a slender girl with curly brown hair. "Don't think I would have lasted long on the surface. After all, can't really hide what I look like!" His voice held a joking tone, but I caught a sense of fear as well.

"Well, I'm very glad she found you." I knew the fate my friend would have faced had he remained on the surface.

"Me too. Plus, it's *so* much cooler down here. Don't have to deal with the sun. And no fear of leftover radiation."

I rolled my eyes. "Oh please, it's been sixteen years since the war! And we didn't even get hit."

Caleb chuckled. "Okay, surface rat. Enjoy your heat."

I gave a small laugh, rolling my eyes again. Before I could respond, Caleb pointed toward Kailey and Max.

"Did they instantly find you?"

I gulped, feeling my smile drop. *How was I supposed to tell him without bringing up Olivia?* I was painfully aware I'd eventually have to tell him what happened, but that conversation could wait.

"Oh, no." I shook my head, thinking through how to shorten my story. "Like you, I just kept running. I reached some of the suburbs, where I was on my own for a little bit. Then I stumbled upon them."

"Guess we both got lucky then. Couldn't imagine survivin' for too long on my own." I felt a sense of relief when he didn't ask about Olivia's whereabouts. Longing to change the subject, I quickly piped up before he could say more.

"Have you been to an Uprising meeting before?"

"Plenty of times!" He straightened up a bit. "I've even had the honor to participate in some of the attacks. It feels great to fight back, to give those bastards a taste of their own medicine."

"This will be my first ever meeting." I stepped over a large crack in the ground. "I'm a bit nervous but looking forward to it."

"Oh, you have nothing to be nervous about," Caleb reassured me. "And besides, they've gotten so big no one will know you're new. We'll be lost in the crowd soon." Caleb smiled as we turned a corner into a brightly lit hallway. Up ahead was another group of people, their clothes just as ragged.

We continued chatting as the hallways got louder and more crowded. We passed a few rooms and other hallways, some of which contained other groups. We eventually entered a large, bright room with white walls and artificial plants. I glanced around in amazement at the size of the crowd, staying close to Caleb. As the room filled up, I felt my nervousness fading. With my friends surrounding me, I was ready for my first Uprising meeting.

Chapter Twenty-Nine

"I want to learn!" Jennifer leaped closer to Max and Sid who were pretend boxing in preparation for tonight's Uprising attack. Annie stayed close to her sister as Sid dodged a punch from Max. The two laughed as Sid knocked out Max's legs, declaring her victory as Annie and Jennifer climbed on top Max and pinned him to the ground. Luckily for him, the ground was the soft carpet of the downstairs basement.

"I don't think that's fair now," Chester chuckled from where the rest of the group watched. "Three against one?"

"I can take it!" Max said, sitting up. As he did so, Annie playfully knocked him back down.

"You sure about that?" Elliot snickered.

"More like, he *can't* take it," Kailey added as the group laughed.

"I'd like to see you try!" Max retorted as the twins continued holding him down.

As Max and the twins carried on, my thoughts drifted to Caleb. Seeing him the other night had greatly improved my mood, and the Uprising meeting had pumped me up for tonight's attack. I wondered how Caleb was preparing for this evening. *Do others practice fighting like us?* Tonight's attack was predicted to be a major one since we would descend upon a government building in Center City. It would be a risky night, but I was ready for it.

Carlotta came to my side. "You sure you're up for this?" she whispered, her voice sweet as usual. "No one will think any less of you if you don't go."

I met her gaze as Kailey entered the fight to aid Max against the twins and Sid. The five of them, along with Carlotta and me, would be participating in the attack. "I appreciate it," I muttered back. "But I'm ready for this."

She nodded. "Just wanted to check."

I smiled briefly at her before turning my attention back to the fighting. With Kailey on his side, Max had finally gotten off the floor. I chuckled, feeling confident my companions would be unparalleled tonight as the pretend fight came to an end.

Sid made her way to her collection of journals in one of the cabinets as the others plopped down, taking deep breaths. "I have a poem I wanna share!" she said, pulling open a notebook.

"Well, let's hear it," Chester said as the group turned to face where she stood behind some bean bag chairs.

"It's called 'Let's be Rebels'," Sid said, propping the book up in her arms. After clearing her throat, she read loudly:

"There comes a time we must understand something very important.

We are more than our bodies.

Sure, those may be your arms and your legs,

Your cute little nose and your silly ears,

Your sweet smile that can light up a room.

But we are more than the numbers.

More than the number on the scale,

The number of pimples on our cheeks,

More than the scars hidden under layers.

We are more than the hair we dye.

We are more than the contacts they force us to use.

We are the smiles we give to others

We are the compassion we show a struggling friend

We are the kindness shown to a stranger who needed it most.

Human complexity could never be captured from the exterior.

Our bodies are temporary

The soul is forever.

The physical was no choice,

But the internal can be mended.

Over and over again, to be as beautiful as possible.

Because in a world obsessed with external features,

A world that only considers some worthy,

Let's be rebels

And nourish and love our souls, and the souls of each other.

Over and over again

Until unconditional love and self-worth are found from within,

And not from the superficial side of society."

As she finished up, the basement erupted into claps and cheers. Sid bowed her head then tucked her journal back into the cabinet, her cheeks turning slightly red.

"Sid, that was great!" I said as the claps died down.

"Indeed, it was!" Max added.

"Remember us when you're famous!" Kailey joked, still clapping.

Annie and Jennifer rushed forward to hug her, nearly pulling the girl to the ground. "Our rockstar!" the twins chanted over and over again as Sid attempted to take a few steps forward.

I felt a wide smile spread across my lips as the group continued to praise Sid for her skills. As the chatter died down and those of us joining the Uprising attack got our shoes on, I felt a rush of happiness and excitement spread through my veins. *Bring it on, regulators! I* thought as we exited the basement. *We're fearless rebels and we're coming for ya!*

Chapter Thirty

"Stay down!" Sid called from up ahead. We moved through a dark alleyway, emerging from the tunnels alongside others in the Uprising. The crowd was massive. I stayed close to my friends to avoid getting lost in it.

I came to Sid's side as some of the Uprising advanced forward. The stars glistened overhead, and a warm breeze stirred through the mass of people. I occasionally glanced over my shoulder to make sure the rest of my group was keeping pace. Max and Kailey were right behind us, and following closely were Carlotta and the twins, one holding each of Carlotta's hands. Beyond them were people I didn't recognize but yet was willing to perish alongside tonight in the fight for a better world. *I'm fighting for what's right,* I thought in an attempt to settle my racing heart. I placed my hand over my pocket containing Olivia's barrette. *And also, in memory of Olivia.*

"We're getting close!" A whisper stirred through the crowd. I glanced around as we pressed on. I hadn't yet spotted Caleb among the multitude of people. I prayed silently for his safety, as well as God's protection to be over all those fighting tonight.

After a few more twists and turns, we peered around the skyscrapers at a massive marble building with large columns and a dome. The building was huge, but I felt sure we could easily overtake it.

"Such a pretty building," Max whispered right before we descended with the rest of the Uprising. He scrunched up his nose. "Too bad it's tainted with evil."

The Uprising quickly filed into the building's interior, which held a large entry room lined with various hallways. I watched in amazement as some of the Uprising threw hand grenades down hallways, directed at groups of regulators. Others tackled regulators to the ground, punching and kicking with all their might. I covered my ears, accompanying Max as he knocked a regulator off his feet. I swung my arms, punching the regulator square in the gut before turning to face another who was pulling me back. Almost instinctively, I struck her under the jaw, which caused her to tumble backward. I kicked out her legs, towering over her as she fell with a loud crash onto the hard tile floor.

"That's for killing my sister!" I roared as she whimpered away. Almost as soon as the words escaped my mouth, another regulator dove in my direction. I ducked, sliding sideways to avoid him. Max turned around, quickly striking the regulator from behind as I punched the man's neck. The two of us backed the regulator into a corner, kicking and punching relentlessly while doing our best to avoid the regulator's swinging fists. Pain surged through me as the regulator struck my shoulder. Through clenched teeth, I swung at him with my other arm while Max knocked out his legs. Knowing he had been defeated, the regulator retreated down a dim hallway.

"You good?" Max turned to face me. A bruise was beginning to swell under his right eye.

I nodded, catching my breath as my pulse pounded in my ears. The two of us rushed back to the scene, leaping at a regulator that had Jennifer pinned to the ground.

"Get off her!" Max spat out, doing his best to drag the regulator off our young friend. I grabbed the regulator, tugging him away as Max did the same alongside me. Annie quickly rushed forward to give her sister a helping hand while Max and I fought off the regulator.

I glanced around once the regulator sprinted off. I spotted Carlotta not too far away, fighting a regulator around her size. With a final punch, she sent the regulator running. Kailey and Sid fought farther down. They wrestled alongside others in the Uprising against a tide of regulators that formed a tight wall. Some of the regulators pushed against the wave of unworthies with shields while others struggled against the punches and kicks of the Uprising. Some of the Uprising slashed swords while others stood a bit off, firing arrows into the sea of regulators. A hand grenade was tossed into the side containing regulators, causing some of the wall to crumble and a few regulators to fall down, allowing the Uprising to advance even more. As more and more regulators fled the room, I felt a smile creep across my face. *We've got this! We're really going to win!*

I rushed to Kailey's side, pushing with all my might against a regulator shield as they advanced. Sid pushed against another shield to my right.

"Don't let up!" A voice sounded above the clashing. I couldn't tell which side it came from.

I locked eyes with Sid as the shield moved back about an inch. Her eyes were wide, but I caught a glimmer of hope within them. I looked back at the regulator, taking the opportunity to kick his groin as hard as I could when he lifted his shield slightly.

Yes!

I felt my hope dwindle as more regulators emerged from the hallways with guns drawn. Loud bangs and a white smoke began to fill the space. I fell back with a cough as smoke gathered around me.

"Come on!" Kailey grabbed my shirt, pulling me to my feet. I reached through the smoke hoping to find Sid, but was quickly dragged away empty-handed.

Shouts reached my ringing ears as Kailey and I stumbled through the packed space. Blood splattered on the white floor and bodies fell.

I blinked, my eyes starting to burn and swell with tears. Through blinks, I caught a glimpse of Max rushing toward us. Kailey slowly let go of me.

"We . . . we left Sid!" I cried, letting out another cough. "We have to go back!"

"I can't find the others!" Max yelled through the noise as he reached our side. He let out a few deep coughs into his elbow.

The three of us rushed to a corner, ducking smoke and bullets and falling bodies. I scanned around the chaos-filled room, feeling sick as the white floor began to flow red. *Where are they?*

"There!" I pointed to a regulator that had a firm grip on the twins. They wrestled against him, attempting to break free as tears streamed down their freckled faces. Max instantly rushed forward, Kailey and me right behind him.

"Let them go!" Kailey yelled as she lunged at the regulator. Max grabbed on to Annie, attempting to pull her loose while I did the same to Jennifer. I stumbled back, arms securely around the twin as I ripped her out of the regulator's grip.

"Annie!" She wailed, instantly springing up to help her sister. I climbed to my feet but was quickly knocked back down as Max landed on top of me, painful screams escaping his mouth.

"No, no, no!" I cried out as his white shirt began to turn red. Wrapping my arms around him, I dragged him away from the regulator who pointed his gun at us. I pulled Max backwards, Kailey eventually reappearing at our side with her arms around Jennifer. Kailey held the girl securely as she thrashed against her, screaming for her twin.

The four of us made our way to the entrance of the building, retreating with others in the Uprising as regulators continued to advance. Through the smoke, I spotted some regulators disappearing into the building's halls, dragging members of the Uprising with them. My heart sank as I noticed Annie, Sid, and Carlotta among them.

The remaining four of us, Max, Kailey, Jennifer, and me, stayed still and silent for a moment as we watched our friends get dragged deeper into the building's interior, then without a word, we exited the building alongside the rest of the Uprising.

Oh Lord, please let them be okay!

Chapter Thirty-One

"I can help," Jennifer offered, coming to my side. "Really, I'm okay."

The four of us stumbled through an old neighborhood. Max had his arms stretched out, securely on Kailey's and my shoulders. We carried him steadily as we made our way back home, careful to take it slow and easy so as to minimize the bleeding. He was silent except for an occasional whimper. This was the quietest he'd ever been.

"Just stay close," I pleaded, not wanting to lose anyone else. She had already been struggling to keep up, pausing at times to glance back as if she couldn't bear the thought of leaving her sister behind. "And please try to keep the lantern steady." The bright lantern swung carelessly at her side.

"My nose won't stop running," Jennifer said with a sniffle.

"It'll be okay," Kailey said, the three of us turning a corner. She blinked her eyes constantly as if they were irritated. "We've got tissues back home, and we're almost there."

I felt my stomach churn as the old house came into view through the darkness. As we got closer, my thoughts drifted to the story of Jordyn. Carlotta's words stirred through me as we staggered down the street. *'We tried carrying her back home, but it was too late. She lost too much blood, and we weren't able to save her.'* I shook the thoughts away as Husker rushed to meet us.

"I got him, I got him!" he said, taking Max into his arms. Max grunted as he was transferred and rushed inside. The rest of the group quickly came to meet us as we entered, inspecting us for injuries.

"Lay him down!" Chester instructed Husker, who placed Max gently on the basement's old red couch. Trevor rushed into his bedroom, re-emerging with a box of supplies as the rest of us gathered around the couch. Elliot came to my side, placing his hand on my shoulder.

"What happened?" Chester asked, not taking his eyes off Max. Slowly, he lifted up Max's shirt to reveal a bullet wound. He fished through the box of supplies as Kailey stepped forward.

"The Uprising had to retreat," she said as Chester began to patch up Max's wound. Max hissed through clenched teeth as Chester wiped down the area. "They were shooting at us, and taking people hostage ..." She broke off as Max let out a scream.

"They took Carlotta. And Sid, and Annie." I finished for her. "We tried to save them, but we couldn't."

Chester paused briefly, glancing up. "Where did they take them?" His voice was firm but still had his usual hint of gentleness, similar to Carlotta's tone. *Oh please, please Lord!* I cried silently as I thought of our leader. *Please don't let the regulators hurt her or the others!*

I shook my head. "Just deeper into the building, down the hallways."

"It was hard to see clearly," Kailey chimed in, rubbing her eyes. "The regulators used tear gas to disperse us."

"Go wash up," Chester commanded, continuing to patch up Max. Kailey and Jennifer quickly bounded away. I followed a bit more slowly, my eyes glued to Max. *Please Lord, let him be okay!* Elliot removed his hand from my shoulder as I turned to leave, trailing behind me slowly.

"Are you okay?" Elliot asked as we climbed the steps.

I nodded slightly. "I think so . . . still taking it all in. I don't know if it's sunk in yet."

"I'll grab some clean clothes for you to change into once you're done," Elliot offered as we reached the bathroom. Kailey and Jennifer sat on the rim of the tub, still fully clothed. I watched as Kailey turned on the facet slowly before wiping down Jennifer's arms and face with a rag.

"Thank you," I breathed out as he hurried down the hallway. Kailey handed me a rag as I joined them. The warm water circled around my toes as I swung my legs into the tub. I instantly splashed some on my face, blinking slowly to ensure some of it cleaned out my eyes. The burning had faded but I wanted to make sure I cleaned everything thoroughly. Kailey handed me a large container of soap, and I quickly started to wipe down my exposed arms and legs.

"I'm sorry," Kailey whispered as she dragged a wet rag over her arms. "Usually, attacks don't go so badly. I'm sorry we dragged you into that." Her voice was barely audible.

I sighed, rinsing my rag under the water. "It's not your fault. You don't have to feel bad about anything." I pulled the wet rag down my soapy arms, allowing the water to flow down my arms and into the tub.

Jennifer slowly got off the tub's side, placing her rag and towel where she once sat. "I'm going to check on Max," she said before disappearing into the hall.

I turned to Kailey, who was drying herself off with a towel. I grabbed a towel for myself after rinsing off my legs. "How are we going to get them back?"

She pressed her lips together, her eyes narrowing. "I'm not sure," she replied. "No one has ever been taken before."

"I have!" She glanced over at me in surprise. "Well, before I got here. The regulators took us to a station where they locked us up."

"There's only station four left. The Uprising took out the rest."

"Then let's go!"

"Oliver," Kailey's voice was stern. "We just got back, and we nearly lost Max as well. We have to regain our strength, and there's no certainty we'd be able to successfully break them out."

I paused briefly from drying myself off, knowing she was right. We had to rest up first and we needed support if we were to succeed. I breathed out deeply, setting my rag and towel alongside the ones Jennifer had used.

"Chester's in charge now," Kailey said, rolling up her towel. "Let's talk things over with him."

Chapter Thirty-Two

"We'll send some forces to station four first. There's a possibility many of our people are being held there, and we need to train better and gather more forces before going after Center City again. I do not want to lose any more of my people."

Kailey and Chester shifted beside me as we listened intently to Harriet, the leader of the Uprising. We had learned of this meeting only hours prior after I had checked in with Caleb, who sat next to me now in the crowded tunnel. The two had tagged along with me to check in with the underground group, where we learned the Uprising was planning an emergency meeting after the failed attack a few days ago. I had been delighted to know I was not alone in wanting to strike back and free those who were taken.

"Pass on the news to your groups," Harriet continued. "Messengers, please spread the word to groups not present. We will meet at sundown tomorrow as decided. Go in peace, for our meeting together has ended. And do not forget how much the future depends on us."

Caleb got to his feet as the meeting concluded. Kailey, Chester, and I quickly followed. The four of us exited the room alongside some others.

"I'm glad you're okay," I said to Caleb as we walked on through the tunnels. "Did your group lose many people?"

"Just Catherine and Matt. I'm eager to get them both back."

"I'm sure you are," Kailey spoke up. "I'm ready to beat up every regulator I see until they give us back our sweet Annie and my Sid and Carlotta!"

"We'll get them back," Chester said as we emerged into the tunnel Caleb and his group dwelt in. "I promise."

"Well, you three better get home, it'll be gettin' dark soon," Caleb mentioned. "And thank you for checking in, I really appreciate it."

"Of course," I said, giving my friend a hug. "Wanted to make sure you were okay."

"Stay safe, Caleb," Chester said as the three of us turned to leave our comrade. "See you again soon."

Caleb nodded, then the three of us left the tunnels, the sun's rays illuminating the evening sky as we made our way back home.

***

"I think . . ." Jennifer trailed off, staring intently at my clenched fist. "Your marble is red!" She smiled at me as she made her decision.

I chuckled, opening my palm to expose a dark blue marble. "Not even close!"

She scrunched up her nose as she gazed at the marble in disbelief. "Not fair! I've been guessing them all right!"

Max stirred on the couch behind us. "Oliver's probably got a red one up his sleeve." It was refreshing to watch my friend return to his jokester ways as he healed, but it had become evident he was *not* on my side during this game. He watched us closely, ensuring neither of us cheated. Trevor sat beside him, motioning with his hand for Max to lie back down and relax. The boy had been leaving his room more often to tend to Max, hoping his knowledge from healing his own wound would help. He watched over our game closely, a large grin on his face.

Elliot narrowed his eyes from where he sat beside me. "Perhaps I should check," he smirked, reaching for my arm.

Trevor snickered. "Yeah, I bet there's some up there!"

"Hey!" I snatched my arm away from Elliot, shaking out the sleeves. "See? I don't have anything!"

"For now," Elliot sneered, pulling his arm back. Max huffed as I placed the marble back into the bag. I turned away, closing my eyes tightly as Jennifer picked one out for me to guess. I didn't see much of a point to this game, but Jennifer had been begging for someone to play with her all morning. I had given in after finishing my breakfast.

"Okay!" Jennifer said, signaling for me to open my eyes. I leaned forward, peering through her closed fingers in the hope of spotting any color. She held her fist slightly above the carpet as I debated what color marble was hiding underneath. We had all the colors of the rainbow in the bag, and she had already picked out red, blue, and green marbles.

"Hmm . . . I'm thinking either yellow or purple, but I'm not sure."

"You have to pick one!" Jennifer exclaimed, not releasing her grip.

"I'm thinking you may want to go with yellow," Max chimed in, raising an eyebrow playfully.

"Definitely yellow," Elliot added.

I rolled my eyes. "Purple!" I laughed slightly as Elliot chuckled. "I'm not listening to you all again!" They had already made me guess the wrong color twice.

Jennifer giggled, opening her hand to reveal a purple marble.

"Yes!" I cheered. I nudged Elliot playfully then glared at Max, who was struggling to hold back his laughter. "You all were trying to set me up!" I wanted to playfully nudge Max as well, but I held back. He had been getting better, but he was still in pain. The last thing I wanted to do was add to it.

"Don't know why you listened to them in the first place," Trevor teased.

"I still can't tell whose side you're on!" I chuckled.

Jennifer dropped her marble back into the bag then climbed to her feet. "I'm done playing now. I'm going to get food."

"Alrighty then," I said as she exited the basement, the rest of us still laughing. Elliot quietly got up, bits of laughter still escaping him.

"I'll catch you all later," he said as he left the space, presumably to grab some food as well.

"Same," Trevor said, heading for his room.

I sealed the bag of marbles tightly after getting the rest of my laughter out. "So," I turned to Max. "You feeling any better?"

"It's been a lot better." He lay back down as I stirred to my feet. "I can't wait to be fully recovered. That way I can fight again."

"You'll get there before you know it." I wasn't sure how much longer it would take him, but the progress each day felt miraculous. The Lord had been quick to answer my prayers and thankfully the bullet had not burrowed too deep.

"That's right," he whispered, shutting his eyes. Assuming he wanted some alone time to rest, I quietly made my way out of the space.

"Hey, Oliver?"

I turned, quickly returning back to his side. "Yes?"

"Thank you." His voice was gentle, something unusual for him. "For helping carry me back home and checking on me daily. You've really proven yourself; you fought well, and I know you'll do great tonight." He paused briefly, stirring on the couch. "I'm proud to have you by my side."

Wow, a compliment from Max? I smiled. It was rare to receive a compliment from Max, so I knew his words were not empty praise. "The feeling is mutual, Max. I'll be sure to fill you in on every detail once we get back."

He smirked. "Good. Now go kick some regulator ass for me."

I grinned. "Will do!" As I left the space, I felt a fire burning inside me to not only save those taken from us and avenge Olivia, but also to avenge Max. I held my head high as I placed the marbles back on a shelf. I was ready to prove my abilities once again tonight.

Chapter Thirty-Three

I peered through the shrubs to get a better view of the regulator station. It was just as boring and ugly as the one Olivia and I had been taken to. I turned away from the station to look at the sheer mass of people that had gathered with us. Countless numbers associated with the Uprising had met us as the sun set. I watched as Chester and Kailey moved through the crowd, greeting those who had just arrived. They stopped briefly to talk to Harriet and a few others I recognized from the last Uprising meeting. Jennifer followed them, her head held high.

I sighed, turning to Elliot who returned my gaze. I had so much I wanted to say but when I opened my mouth, the words failed to come out.

"You feeling up to this?" Elliot whispered as I looked away.

"Yeah!" I plucked the grass below, praying my friend could not tell just how rapid my breath was becoming. Thankfully, I could hide in the darkness as the day faded. "Are you?"

"Always am." I could feel his eyes watching me intently as I took out Olivia's barrette and began to fidget with it. *I wish you were here, Liv!* Taking some deep breaths, I met his gaze once more with a small smile.

"I'll be okay." It was obvious he knew. "Really, I'll be okay," I repeated as the crowd stirred. I felt his hand lightly on my shoulder as we climbed to our feet.

"It's okay to be a bit scared, Oliver," he whispered. "I think we all are. But you don't need to push your fear away. Lean into it, and allow it to push you to fight for what's right, what you believe in." He paused briefly, nodding toward the rest of the group as they came to our side. "And remember, we'll be right with you every step of the way."

I stayed silent, swallowing the lump in my throat. *It's going to be okay*, I thought in an attempt to reassure myself. *Just lean into the memories instead of shaking them away.* I felt strength rise within me as I started to push past the vegetation and run with the others. I clutched the barrette tightly, careful not to drop it.

"Thanks, Elliot," I muttered out as we crossed the fence before erupting into the station with the rest of the Uprising. *Time to avenge you, Olivia!* I thought, sliding her barrette back into my pocket.

The inside of the station was dull with flickering lights. Glass shards began to cover the floor as members of the Uprising broke through doors and windows, quickly overtaking the guards. Shouts and screams pierced the air, but none compared to the shrill noise from the overhead alarms or occasional hand grenades thrown by the Uprising.

Covering my ears, I followed Chester, Elliot, and Jennifer down a crowded hall. People emerged from their cells as locks clanked to the ground alongside the broken glass. I ducked through the crowd, careful to not lose sight of my companions as they peeked into each cell in search of our friends. A wall crumbled as another grenade went off, kicking up smoke and debris as regulators fell to the ground.

"They're not down here!" Chester called out from farther down the hallway.

"We'll try a different one!" Jennifer turned on her heels, fleeing in the opposite direction. The rest of us ran after her, Kailey rejoining us as we burst through a set of doors into another hallway.

Although not nearly as crowded as the first hallway, this one was bustling with noise and excitement too as the Uprising freed individuals from their cells. My eyes scanned through the crowd as my heart jolted into my throat. *Oh please, appear soon!* The ringing in my ears felt unbearable, and I felt my blood pulsing through me as a regulator knocked down a member of the Uprising. I lunged at the regulator, instantly wrapping my hands around his throat. Kailey knocked out his legs as I did so, and the bulky regulator fell to the ground. The Uprising member nodded at us before pinning the regulator down.

"Go!" he shouted, beads of sweat beginning to collect on his forehead. "Go find your friends. I'll hold him off!"

I released my grip, dashing down the hall after Kailey. The two of us eventually caught up with the others in a hallway lined with rooms instead of cells. The five of us went from room to room, most rooms containing absolutely nothing. The station was quieter in this area, and I felt my chest starting to rise and fall normally as my breath steadied. The sound of alarms and grenades felt far off now.

"Sid!" Jennifer cried, peering through the glass window of a door ahead. The rest of us raced to her side, instantly breaking down the door and entering the large room full of old desks and scattered papers. Sid walked toward us as we entered the room, her eyes wide and her hair sticking out at all angles.

Yes! A smile crept across my lips and relief washed over me. *Thank you, Lord!* It felt amazing to see my friend alive and well. As I looked her over, I felt myself relax. She appeared untouched with no visible injuries.

My shoulders dropped as I noticed her arms. *The regulators must have taken her bracelets.* She looked so bare without them.

Jennifer sprinted forward, wrapping her arms around Sid with a large grin. "We found you!"

"Hey . . ." Sid wiped away tears as we gathered around her. She hugged Jennifer tightly.

"You okay?" Elliot asked in-between breaths.

She nodded slightly, meeting each of our eyes. "Better now." She sniffled, managing a small smile. "I didn't think I'd get out of this place." Her voice was soft, almost a whisper as she struggled to keep her composure. Jennifer hugged her tighter as the rest of us embraced them in a group hug. I remembered just how hopeless I had felt when I was in her shoes. As we each pulled back from the hug, I felt warmth spread through my body to have found such a special chosen family.

"Have you seen Annie?" Jennifer's wail returned me back to the present.

"Or Carlotta?" Chester chimed in.

Sid lifted a brow. "They're . . . they're not with you all?"

Before any of us could respond, a few others trickled into the room.

"Caleb!" I took a few steps toward my friend, who was flanked by others from the Uprising.

"The station's fallen. There's no one else bein' held here," he answered, breathing heavy.

"Fallen?" Elliot repeated.

A girl next to Caleb nodded. "The regulators are fleeing or surrendering."

"You all searched every room? We're still missing some of our crew!" I felt my chest tightened. *If Annie and Carlotta aren't here, then where are the regulators keeping them?* All the other stations had already been taken out by the Uprising. *This is the last station; they have to be here!*

This time a man stepped forward. "Other groups are missing people, too." He looked much older than the rest of us. "They aren't being held here."

"We'll find them," Caleb reassured me, coming to my side. "There's still Center City."

I nodded, casting my gaze down as my heart remained heavy. *I want all of our group to be safe, back home and far away from the regulators,* I thought. I reluctantly followed the others out of the room, sighing deeply as we emerged into halls full of cheer and chatter. I had no desire to take part in the celebration as my thoughts drifted to Carlotta and Annie. Jennifer dragged her feet alongside me, her head hung low.

We'll find them, I silently reassured her, recalling how lost I'd felt at first without Olivia. *I promise.*

Chapter Thirty-Four

I licked my finger to better turn the Bible's pages, which seemed to stick together. I turned around sharply as the back door opened. Sid slowly stepped out, one of her notebooks tucked securely under her arm. Without a word, she sat down next to me at the edge of the patio, her expression unreadable.

"Which book are you reading?" She leaned closer to see the page.

I moved the Bible so we could share it. "Nehemiah. I just finished chapter four."

She nodded, scanning the page and also her notes on the side. "Yes," she said with a smile. "I remember this one!"

I glanced over her as she read the page. She had been quieter than usual these past few days. "They didn't hurt you, did they?"

My heart dropped as she lost her smile and cast her gaze down and away. "I mean," I quickly spoke up, "you don't have to answer that. I was just . . . worried. I know how rough and mean the regulators can be."

She sighed. "No, it's okay. I'd wonder the same." She was quiet for a few more seconds. "They were definitely . . . rough with me." She traced her fingers over her bare arms. "They returned my clothes after they were done with me, but not my bracelets."

Her words hit me like a punch in the gut. I felt tears form in the corners of my eyes as I realized what had happened to her. *No, Lord! I thought. Please protect Annie and Carlotta! Don't let the regulators touch either of them!*

"Sid," I softly breathed out. "I'm so sorry. You didn't deserve that, and I hope you know it's not your fault. I'm sorry we didn't get to you sooner."

Sid gave a small smile, her gaze still cast downward. "A part of me didn't want to fight back," she whispered, her voice barely audible. "It's actually something I've been feeling pretty convicted about, if you don't mind listening?"

"What's on your mind?"

She breathed in deeply before starting. "I just couldn't stop thinking about Jesus and how He never fought back. Even when they mocked Him and hurt Him, even when He went to die. He didn't fight back, and He even prayed for those hurting Him! So, I didn't want to fight back, either. I didn't want to stoop to the level of the regulators. I didn't want to be like them. I wanted to be better than them." She paused briefly, looking at me with sad eyes. "I . . . I wanted to be like Christ."

"But Jesus also flipped the tables," I pointed out. "And Jesus was very stern with the religious authorities who were not kind to others."

She nodded slightly. "I guess you're right. But I still don't want to hurt anyone. Doesn't feel right as a Christian."

"And we're not! Here . . ." I inched the Bible closer to her and pointed to the end of verse fourteen and began to read out the passage. "'Don't be afraid of them. Remember the Lord, who is great and awesome, and *fight* for your families, your sons and your daughters, your wives and your homes.' Sid, we're all fighting for our homes and our families, our friends and our futures, against an oppressive authority that doesn't even think we are worthy of life! God may not want us to be violent people, but we're allowed to defend ourselves and fight for what's right."

Sid stayed still, reading over the rest of the chapter. "Our God will fight for us," she softly whispered out. As I glanced back down at the page, I realized she was quoting the twentieth verse.

"That's right." I prayed the Nehemiah passage was at least offering some reassurance to her. "All of us in the Uprising are fighting for what we believe in, what we know to be right. Jesus understands our situation, and I feel certain He would've understood if you'd fought back. Don't let the regulators get away with hurting you like that."

She met my gaze with a small smile. "Thank you, Oliver. I just wish Carlotta and Annie were here." She paused for a moment, drawing in a deep breath. "She was knitting for me, Carlotta was. She was making me a rainbow scarf."

I thought about the half-finished knitting project that still sat on one of the bunk beds. Carlotta's bunk remained exactly as she had left it. No one had touched the area, leaving the lower bunk frozen in time.

I straightened back up as I cleared my throat.

"We're going to find them." My words sounded strong, but I wasn't so sure. My hope dwindled as the days passed. "They'll be back home before we know it. Then we will all be safe again."

"I hope you're right," she said, opening her notebook.

I leaned closer, closing the Bible. "You draw or write anything lately?"

"I wrote a poem after; I think as a way to cope with what happened." Her gaze met mine with a small smile. "Wanna hear it?"

"I'd love to."

She cleared her throat before beginning. Speaking slowly and clearly, she read:

"From the womb You created me

Fearfully and wonderfully (Psalm 139:14)

Bearing Your very image (Genesis 1:27).

I am so small before You, Lord

Just a little bit of dust (Psalm 103:14).

Dust You could wipe out in a second

You could wipe us all out

But that would break Your heart, for even though we make mistakes,

Even through our failure,

You remain love (1 John 4:8 & 4:16).

You stay patient and understanding,

Far more than any other.

I reveal all to You,

I withhold not one secret from You, Lord.

You are my closest confidant and best friend.

I show You the worst parts of me, revealing those most damaged.

For it is You whom I trust, even with my darkness.

Even with this brokenness, I remain Your child.

I trust You will never abandon me (Hebrews 13:5).

Here I am, all of me before You.

I am small in Your presence.

I am vulnerable.

I am honest.

I am me.

I confess all I am,

Including that which they claim You will hate.

Yet no hate flows from You

As I am wrapped up in love Himself (1 John 4:16).

No reason is enough for You to leave me.

Oh Lord, it is You my heart rejoices in!

It is You whom my trust is in!

I am Yours forever, may Your will be done through me.

May my life be proof of Your unconditional and unwavering love

Extending to *all* Your children.

I am Your child, this I know and trust,

As sure as I know that You love me."

After reading her latest poem, she closed her notebook and looked at me with a smile.

I sat silently for a moment as her words sunk in. "That was beautiful," I finally muttered out, feeling a bit lost to find the right words. "God definitely gave you a powerful gift when it comes to art. Thank you for sharing with me."

"You're welcome!" She beamed, looking very pleased with herself. She glanced off to the distance as I remained silent. Almost as soon as she did, she jumped up with wide eyes, tucking her journal once again under her arm.

"Someone's coming!" she shrieked as I climbed to my feet. I clutched the Bible tightly to my chest as I caught sight of a small figure in the distance. The individual weaved through the abandoned houses, heading straight for ours. As they got closer, I spotted ragged clothes and curled braids. *That's not a regulator . . .*

"Oliver, come on!" Sid yanked my arm, pulling me toward the house.

I shook her off. "Wait!" I blinked in confusion as I started to recognize the approaching girl. "I know her!"

Sid stopped, letting go of my arm. She stood close to my side as the girl crossed the overgrown grass of our backyard. Across her chest was an old brown bag and tucked into her braided hair was the small blue hair clip I remembered so well.

"Nevaeh?" I breathed out in disbelief.

She smiled wide. "It's good to see you again!"

Sid glanced at her nervously. "What's going on? Who are you!?"

"It's okay! I'm with the Uprising," Nevaeh replied calmly. "I'm a messenger. Your messenger hasn't stopped by in a while, so they sent me to check up on you all."

"How did you find us?" I asked, my muscles growing tense. *Were we not as hidden as I'd thought? Was it possible for those outside the group to locate our little safe haven?* The possibility of others discovering us made me shiver. *What if the regulators found us?*

Nevaeh looked amused at my question. "The street signs are still standing, silly. Messengers know how to get to each group. It's a way to keep tabs on each other and communicate."

I felt myself relax at her answer. *Messengers!* I slowly began to remember Harriet mentioning them at a meeting, but I hadn't thought about their role at all. *Okay, we're still hidden from regulators*, I thought with a sigh of relief. "But then, who's our messenger?"

"It's Max." Sid stepped forward. "He's been injured, but he's getting better. We appreciate the check in."

As she replied, I thought about how Max often left in the late evening without saying anything to anyone. *So that's what he was doing all those nights.*

Nevaeh nodded. "Of course. I also came to inquire if you all will be joining the Center City attack. That's our last building to take out, and we suspect many of our people are being held hostage there."

I straightened up. *That must be where Annie and Carlotta are!* "I'm in!" I said without hesitation.

"Me too," Sid spoke up from beside me.

"Excellent!" Nevaeh steadily met our gazes. "We'll be expecting you all then, as well as anyone else from your group who will be joining. The attack will occur three days from now, and some groups are meeting in the tunnels tomorrow evening to train together. You all are free to join that too."

"We'll be glad to," I said as Sid and I glanced at each other. I caught a glimpse of determination in her gaze, and knew she was just as eager as I was to fight. *Perhaps the Nehemiah chapter did help,* I hoped with a smile.

"I'll see you all then," Nevaeh nodded. "Well, I've got other groups to get to before sundown, but it was good to see you again, Oliver. You all take care!"

"Thanks, you too!" I replied as she turned to cross our backyard. Sid nudged me while Nevaeh disappeared into the abandoned neighborhood.

"Come on!" Sid shouted with glee. "Let's go tell the others!"

Chapter Thirty-Five

I strolled down the street without a sound, clutching one of Max's bags tightly to keep it from swinging as it hung off my shoulder. I skipped with excitement once I caught sight of red barns and cottages in the distance. I was aching to meet with the friendly farmers once again.

"Good morning!" A young farmer called out as I approached the wooden table he was sitting at. He looked to be around my age.

"Good morning," I said with a greeting nod. "I've come to visit for a little bit. And if there's any food you'd like to spare, I've come for that too." I felt myself perk up as Martha came around the corner from one of the barns. She smiled in our direction, her face nearly hidden under her large sun hat. In her arms she carried a large watermelon. *I have to get the chance to talk to her!*

"Sure!" the young farmer said. "We've got some vegetables left from the last harvest, and there's some ripe strawberries in that field you're free to pick." He nodded off to a large field with small green plants.

"That would be great, thank you!"

He stirred to his feet. "Okay! I'll go grab some of the leftover veggies now."

I smiled as he disappeared into the nearest barn. While I waited, I watched Martha enter one of the small cottages on the property.

After a few minutes, she emerged from the building into the straw-berry field, beginning to pick and gather what she could into a large wooden basket. *She'll know,* I thought, yesterday's conversation with Sid playing on a loop in my mind. *I'll ask her.*

"Here you go!" The farmer sat down a large wooden crate on the table before me. "Help yourself to as much as you'd like."

"Thank you so, so much." The crate was overflowing with various vegetables, from leafy greens to dusty potatoes to round tomatoes to large squash.

"Yeah, of course! Just leave whatever you don't want here, and I'll be back to get it," the farmer said before entering the nearest field. I quickly filled my bag up with as much as it could hold, casting glances at Martha before wandering toward where she worked. I was careful not to step on any of the plants as I crossed the field.

She paused from her work as I approached, her eyes soft and her smile warm like I remembered. "Well, hello Oliver!" She held out her palm, revealing a plump red strawberry. "Care for a strawberry?"

I took the fruit with a smile, setting my bag down on the ground. "Thanks!" The strawberry was juicy and sweet.

"They're good, aren't they?" Martha plucked a few more, adding them to her basket. "My mother used to call fruit 'God's candy.' If you want to take some home, feel free to."

I swallowed the last of the strawberry, wiping my hand on my pants. "Have you . . . believed in God for long? I noticed you're also a Christian. I even heard you traveled to Jerusalem!"

Martha chuckled. "I've believed for all my fifty years! I was raised by a devout believer, which influenced me quite a bit as I grew." Her cheerful expression and gaze dropped as she continued. "Jerusalem was beautiful and so alive with culture. It's a shame what the war has done — entire kingdoms turned to dust! And I can't comprehend what for." She shook her head, remaining quiet for a bit before meeting my gaze once again. "Is there a reason you ask? Is everything okay?"

I gave a small smile. "It's just . . . I've had some questions lately and I thought it might be good to ask someone a bit older, someone who's walked with God for longer than I have. Someone who would know."

Martha laughed as if amused. "Oh, I'm not sure I'll have the answers you're seeking, but I'm happy to help however I can!" She stooped down to pluck another strawberry. "What's on your mind?"

I cast my gaze down. "Well, my friend and I discussed the Bible recently, and I felt confident in my answer at the time, but now I don't know. I'm scared I'm going to get things wrong, and I don't want to lead people astray! Jesus warned against leading others astray and I believe in Jesus and the Bible, I truly, really do! But what if me just believing isn't enough and I say the wrong things?" I paused briefly, bringing my gaze up to meet hers. Her eyes were full of sympathy. "I'm sorry, I know this is a lot. I just figured you would be a good person to talk to."

Martha smiled as she paused from her work. "Look Oliver, you're young and you're still learning. You're going to get things wrong, that's only human! Jesus *knows* that. He understands we are all flawed, and He *still* loves us. No one has gotten it right all the time, well, no one other than Jesus! He knows you are trying and that you believe, and I think it's wonderful that you and your friend are engaging with the Scriptures. I'm sure you've noticed those in the Bible fail a lot. And yet, God's love and mercy remain. It's not about us and if we get things right all the time; it's about Jesus and the sacrifice He made for us." She paused to pluck another strawberry. "We are saved by grace through faith as Scripture states. I believe that as long as you believe and do your best, you'll be fine."

"But if I get things wrong, isn't that bad?"

"Well, yes! But the good thing is the Holy Spirit will convict you when you make mistakes, when you mess up. And the Spirit will send you to make things right, to seek forgiveness and reconciliation. If you fail, you try again. If you hurt someone, you apologize. If you're doing something bad, like teaching the wrong thing, you'll feel that in your gut and you'll stop."

"And . . . is doing all that enough?" She sat down as I asked my question, leaning back slightly. I slowly sat down next to my bag. The ground was harder than I expected but thankfully not too muddy.

"I believe that's all we can really do, now, isn't it? To do our best to live in peace with others, to improve when we do wrong, and own up to our mistakes. To focus on Jesus, and try to love and serve like He did. He gave us a great example of how to live." She gave a small chuckle. "I certainly don't have all the answers, but I've found that as long as I'm putting Christ first and giving it my best each day, things eventually turn out alright. You'll experience some storms along the way, but Jesus is with you in those. You'll never have to face anything alone with Him."

I grinned. "Like how Jesus calmed the storm when He and the apostles were out at sea!"

Martha leaned closer. "Look at you making connections to Scripture! I think you're doing better than you realize." I felt myself relax at her words, and a sense of confidence rushed through me. Martha's eyes suddenly narrowed as she glanced past me and into the distance. "We do our best but also prepare for the worst, knowing God will bring us the victory, and hopefully soon victory over those scumbags."

I followed her gaze, feeling my heart jump as I spotted a regulator car coming toward the farm. "Quick, Oliver!" Martha grabbed my hand as we rose to our feet. I slung my bag across my shoulder without hesitation. "We'll wait things out inside."

I stayed silent while she rushed me inside one of the cottages — a small space overflowing with piles of boxed produce. The walls and ceilings were stone gray and covered with hanging plants. In the corner stood a small wooden table, and before that, a large tile sink. Along the side of the sink were various vegetables lined up on top of towels, presumably to dry. I inched toward a window, peering out as Martha closed the door behind us.

"What do they want?" I asked, watching a farmer slowly approach the car. I dropped to the floor as the car came to a stop, wrapping my arms securely around my legs while my heart pounded in my chest. My bag plopped down beside me.

"Oh sweetheart, don't worry!" Martha said, crouching down next to me. "You're safe here! They never stick around for long, and they don't come close to our cottages. They just take some produce and go."

I nodded, glancing over at her warm eyes and friendly smile. "Are the other farmers going to be . . . okay? Since they don't look how the regulators want us to look?" I knew I could blend in, but the majority of the farmers I'd come across here could not. *Please, Lord, let them be okay!*

"Yes." Martha's voice was soft but firm. "We keep hats, wigs, and sunglasses on us for this purpose." She peered out the window. "Look at that! The regulators are already getting back in their car! See?" She brought her gaze back to mine. "We're alright." I watched with wide eyes as she got to her feet, still on edge.

"You give them food?" I asked, placing my bag back on my shoulder and slowly climbing to my feet. I took some deep breaths, feeling my heart start to calm down.

"Well, of course! Jesus told us to love our enemies, and Jesus fed Judas! Like I mentioned earlier, we do our best to live like Christ."

"You all do a great job at that!" I smiled as we exited the small building and entered the strawberry field. "You do really good showing the love of Jesus to everyone."

"Oh, thank you! You're so kind." Martha settled back down among the dirt next to her basket, which was now about halfway full. I placed my bag gently on the ground beside it. "But really, I'm just another sinner the Lord shows mercy towards."

I grinned as I sat down next to her, eager to assist in plucking ripe strawberries. "Well, I'm a sinner, too!"

Martha managed a small chuckle before showing me how to determine which strawberries were ready for harvesting and which needed a bit longer. We continued to discuss Jesus and the Bible while we worked on. Even though Martha constantly reassured me she didn't have all the answers, I felt myself relax at her responses as I felt the presence of God wrap around me, shielding me from the blazing sun overhead.

Chapter Thirty-Six

The clashing of metal echoed throughout the fallout shelter as I slouched down against the wall. I panted, folding my legs before me then wrapping my arms tightly around them. This training with the Uprising was much more intense than practice attacks back home. As my breath settled and my muscles relaxed, I looked out over the mass of people that now prepared for the upcoming Center City attack. A variety of shades and tones filled the space. Some wore religious jewelry while others wore religious head coverings. An individual held a cane tightly as they shot out an arrow, landing a bullseye. A bit farther off, a young redhead wrestled against a man with a face similar to Caleb's. My dear friend approached me slowly after winning a bout against a young girl who was using an inhaler before rejoining the practice fighting.

"You doin' alright?" he asked, sitting down next to me.

I managed a small smile. "Just thinking."

Caleb pressed his lips together with a nod. "I get it. We've been through so much and this is a big battle coming up." He perked up slightly. "But soon, it'll all be over. And then we won't have to hide like this."

His words lingered as I continued watching members of the Uprising pretend fight. *Then we won't have to hide.* As my eyes moved from person to person, I could easily pick out what made them unworthy in the eyes of the government. The various disabilities, different hair and eye colors, religious accessories, all stood out. I recalled my morning visit to the farm and how the farmers had to quickly disguise themselves before the regulators.

My thoughts began to race as I considered the people in my life. All of them had to hide their features or something else, like their religion, from the regulators. *Why am I so different?* I pondered. *Why do I look like the city folks? Why do I look the way the regulators and emperor want people to look?*

"I've never had to hide . . ." I glanced over at my friend in shock after realizing I had spoken my thoughts out loud. He returned my gaze with a raised eyebrow. "Well, I mean . . ." I chuckled, hoping I had not offended him. "When I wore my cross necklace, I had to hide that. So of course that made me unworthy according to the government."

"Yes, that's true." His tone was calm, and I felt a sense of relief flood over me. "Is this something you've been thinking about?"

"Not really, at least not since joining the Uprising. Just look." I motioned over the crowd. "Everyone here has to hide. They are *visibly* unworthies." I turned my gaze back to my friend. "But I don't have to hide in any way. When I go into the city, I don't have to cover my eyes or hair like my friends. I'm able to walk around city folks without worry." I paused briefly, thinking back to the orphanage. "Even when I think about the orphanage and growing up, Olivia and I looked so different compared to everyone else! I guess . . . I guess I'm just wondering why I'm so different. Why I'm like the city folks that hate us so much."

Caleb remained quiet for a bit. "No one ever told ya?" he finally muttered out.

"Told me what?"

"We were . . ." He broke off, his eyes widening as he focused on me. He gulped before starting again. "We were dumpster babies. We aren't actually from the orphanage. They just rescued us and raised us as their own."

I sat back against the wall for support as Caleb finished speaking. I saw the people continuing their practice before us, but also saw through them. "Are we even from here? This country, I mean."

Caleb shrugged; his eyes locked on me. "Don't know. All I know is they found us in the rubbish from a government-run shelter. Allegedly, that's where most of the orphanage was found."

"But why would they throw us out?" I felt my stomach drop. "That doesn't make sense! Both Olivia and I were blond and blue-eyed, and we don't have any health issues or disabilities. Plus, they wouldn't have known our sexual orientation since we were just babies then." I paused as my voice cracked. "We're *exactly* what the government wants! They always keep at least one twin according to their policies." I pulled my sister's barrette out of my pocket and traced the butterfly wings gently with my fingers.

"I'm . . . not sure. I mean, look at me!" Caleb giggled. "It's pretty clear why I got thrown out. But either you or Olivia should not have been tossed, especially since you both were healthy and what they want."

I stood up, taking a few steps forward as my mind began to spin. The group's remarks when I first met them rang through my mind. *'They look just like city folks! Like I said, they're twins! You know the government doesn't allow that with their one child policy. They wouldn't have allowed both to live. Those cowards are scared of a big fami-ly challenging them.'* Max and Carlotta's conversation rang through my thoughts. *If Olivia and I were from a big family,* I thought, *we wouldn't even have existed.* City folks were sterilized after their first child to keep families small and preserve resources. *This doesn't make sense!* I continued to ponder over it as Caleb came to my side, his eyes full of concern. *Olivia and I were definitely twins, born at the same time, but why would both of us be thrown out by a government that desired our features?*

I froze as an image of the regulator we had seen during the cat run entered my mind. *No, that can't be right.* I tried to shake the thought away, but the memory of that regulator lingered, as did Trevor's remark about our similarity. I gripped the barrette tightly as my mind connected the dots.

"We weren't just twins . . ." I breathed out, the realization hitting. "We were thrown out because they chose the other one." I paused as tears formed in the corners of my eyes. *This isn't fair; this isn't right!* I wanted to run away, to dash off and escape everything. *This can't be my reality!* I leaned back against the wall for support, not caring to stop my tears. "They chose to save the other triplet." Caleb remained silent, glancing down at the ground as I continued. "Whoever our parents were, they had three blond, blue-eyed babies. But since they were staying in a government shelter . . ."

"They could only keep one." Caleb finished for me as my words stopped coming. I wiped my eyes. It all made sense now, but I felt so empty inside. *Why did they choose him over us? Why weren't Olivia and I good enough?* When Caleb spoke again, his voice was soft. "I'm sorry, Oliver. I wanted you to be the one to say it."

"Did you know?" I didn't like the thought of it possibly being a secret that others at the orphanage kept from us. I felt a sense of relief as Caleb shook his head.

"No, no one told me. But I kind of guessed it. It was all that made sense."

I took a deep breath as I turned back to the Uprising, none of them aware of the storm brewing in my mind. I wiped my tears and sniffled, doing my best to pull myself together. As my eyes narrowed, I felt a fire burning within me. I tucked the barrette back into my pocket, a rush of courage surging through my veins.

"Train me to fight without flaws, Caleb. I'm more than ready to take out this horrid government. After all, the cowards we'll soon be facing didn't just take Olivia from me, but my other wombmate as well. I'm ready for them to experience the pain they've caused me."

Chapter Thirty-Seven

"Yes ma'am. All the groups I met with will have members join."

"Thank you, Nevaeh," Harriet said as the young girl finished reciting her message.

Dallas walked a few feet ahead of them in the tunnel. "That means we will have plenty of forces to take out Center City." He came to a halt once they reached a corner that split into three more tunnels.

"Indeed, we will." Harriet gave a small bow to Nevaeh before the girl exited down one of the tunnels to return to her own group. "We'll have all we need to take power. I've been dreaming of this moment since I was around her age."

"I never thought we'd get this far," Dallas added as they watched Nevaeh disappear before continuing down a different tunnel. "But I knew I saw something in you when you started to speak out against our teachers."

"I couldn't have done it without you, the rest of our friends, and now all these groups that fight alongside us," Harriet confessed. "I'm beyond proud of what we've built together and how far we've come. It feels so surreal."

"It does. I'm glad I stayed."

"I'm glad you did too."

The two continued on in silence, both of them recalling past memories. As they passed through an old fallout shelter, they recognized one of their old classrooms. The desks were still neatly arranged and posters of the emperor that once lined the walls now littered the floor. The two entered the space slowly, Harriet pausing to spin a globe.

"It's so strange. People once lived all over this planet," she said as her fingers traced over continents. "Now all that's left is us. Well, as far as we know. I can't imagine anyone has survived this long out there. If, and that's *if* there're any pockets of survivors out there, they'd have to be far and few." Harriet paused, removing her hand from the globe and glancing up. "But I like our city with the pretty skyline against the night sky, the surrounding forests and wildlife, it's all very nice. I can't wait to fully enjoy it once we take out the emperor and his headquarters tonight."

"It'll be a big battle, that's for sure," Dallas responded. "All the remaining regulators have consolidated to the headquarters, but now, there's more of us then there are of them." After a brief moment of silence, he added, "You going to take out the emperor, if it comes to it? Or would you like me to?"

Harriet remained still for a minute, letting the question fully sink in. She thought of her parents, of her time being raised to worship the emperor in the shelters, and thought of the classmates they'd lost along the way. She drew in a deep breath, straightening up her shoulders.

"We'll see if he surrenders, then we'll decide what to do with him. If he follows the lead of the regulators who surrendered, he'll have to either honor our leadership or flee into the wilderness. I'll give him some choice in the matter. Remember Dallas, you don't have to kill someone to prove you've beaten them."

Dallas raised an eyebrow, letting out a muffled laugh. "You're better than I am then. I won't hesitate if he gives us no choice."

Harriet met his gaze steadily. "Neither will I. But let's hope it doesn't come to too much of a bloodbath tomorrow."

"We'll see," Dallas muttered as the two slowly exited the room.

"That we shall."

Chapter Thirty-Eight

"You ready for tonight, Oliver?"

I stirred under my sheets as Elliot dashed into our shared room. I sat up while he crouched down next to my bed, his smile warm as always.

"You bet!" My quick power nap had rejuvenated my spirit. I wanted to be as energized as possible for the upcoming Center City attack.

"It's hard to believe this may be the final attack. Like, this is it." He wrapped his arms tightly around his legs as he sat down. "This is the final area that needs to fall in order for the Uprising to gain control. It's just . . . hard to imagine everything changing."

"Wouldn't that be great?" I perked up. "You would no longer have to hide. We wouldn't have to live in fear of the regulators!" As cheerful as I was, I couldn't sense the same from my friend. His eyes stared off into space as I spoke, and a short shudder passed through his body. Noticing his expressions, I quickly added, "Are you nervous?"

Elliot gulped before meeting my gaze. "What if we don't win? What if it goes similar to the other time?" His tone was rather quiet.

I grabbed his trembling hand. "Elliot, you're an excellent fighter. You're going to do great and you're so fast! I have no doubts about you or the rest of the Uprising. All of us united like that won't easily be defeated." A smile slowly returned to his face and his hand became still as I continued. "Tonight, I get to avenge Olivia, and possibly my other wombmate as well." Elliot had been the only group member I'd confided in so far regarding being a triplet. "And I know there are people you'd like to avenge too. Tonight, we get to strike back and fight for a world where we can all be free and live under a more equitable government. And if it goes bad, then we try again! And again, and again, for however long it takes. But I have a feeling that things are going to go well tonight. Together, we'll gain the victory and soon, we'll be back home celebrating."

Elliot pulled back his hand slowly. "You know," his tone was soft, "I never imagined I'd have a roommate, or be about to fight against a government! But if I *have* to do those things, I'm glad it's with you."

I felt my face glow red as a warm feeling spread through me. "The feeling is mutual. I never really thought I'd have a roommate who isn't Olivia, but now that I do, I'm thankful it's you."

Before Elliot could respond, Jennifer rushed into the room, crashing on the floor beside us. "Max sent me up. He says it's time to go!" She grabbed on to each of our arms, doing her best to pull us to our feet. "Come on, it's time to save Annie and Carlotta!"

"Alright, we're coming!" I grunted, pretending like she had actually pulled me to my feet.

"You're so strong!" Elliot praised as he pretended to be pulled to his feet as well. "Save some strength for the attack!"

Jennifer giggled before skipping out of our room. As Elliot put on a second sock and his shoes, I considered asking why he preferred to only wear one sock at times. I grabbed Olivia's barrette, stuffing it into my pocket as he entered the kitchen. *I'll ask him after the battle*, I decided, dashing out of the room after him. *We'll have more time to talk then.*

Following my friends into the night, I straightened my back and held my head high. I was beyond ready to fight alongside friends who felt more like siblings and even more ready to be reunited with two of them shortly.

Chapter Thirty-Nine

"Watch out!" I roared as a regulator lunged at Max. My warning caused Max to instantly duck out of reach. He swung with great force, sending the regulator running after hitting him square in the face.

"Thanks for that!" Max exclaimed, racing back to us as the regulator fled. He had decided he was well enough to join the fight, and I was thankful to have him back at my side as the Uprising pressed deeper into the Center City building. We made our way through the battle, covering our ears as grenades went off and on the lookout for Annie and Carlotta.

As we moved from room to room, I also kept my eyes peeled for the regulator who looked like me. *Is he truly my triplet? Is he here?* I couldn't help but wonder what might happen if we ran into each other. *Would he hesitate to hurt me*? I knew it would be hard for me to hurt him. I hoped he shared the same sentiment.

"They aren't in here!" Jennifer called out after peering into a room.

Chester rushed out of another room. "They aren't in here either," he reported.

Sid let a screech as a regulator grabbed her. Kailey and Elliot instantly rushed forward to take on the regulator, the rest of us following.

"Let her go!" I yelled, tugging at the regulator in the hope he would release his grip. As the regulator crashed to the floor, Sid broke free, striking him alongside the rest of us. The man slid back in an attempt to get away, but before he could flee, Chester grabbed his collar.

"Show us where they're keeping a girl that looks like her." He pointed to Jennifer. "And another girl a bit older with golden hair and freckles. Show us where they're holding those they captured last time we stormed this building."

"Never!" The regulator spat out, striking Chester on the side of the head. I felt my blood boil as Chester stumbled back. The rest of us rushed forward, doing all we could to inflict pain on the regulator.

"Where are they!?" Jennifer shouted, digging her nails across the regulator's face as the rest of us punched and kicked the man. "You bastard! Where is my sister!?" The regulator howled in pain as the seven of us overpowered him, successfully pinning him to the ground.

I wrapped my hands tightly around his neck. "Tell us, now!" I trembled as the words escaped my lips. "We could easily kill you, right here, right now! Is that what you want? If not, tell us where our friends are!"

"Some they killed, some are farther down the hall," the regulator grumbled.

I dug my nails into his neck. I wanted nothing more than to end the regulator's life to avenge my wombmates, but the Holy Spirit's conviction stirring within me was too strong to ignore. I thought back to Sid and I's discussion the other day. *If I kill him,* I started to realize, *I'm no better than him.*

"Go," I breathed out, releasing my grip. "You know you have been defeated. We shouldn't have to kill you to prove that."

As the others released their grips, the regulator ran off and disappeared down the hall.

"Come on!" I continued down the hall. "You heard him! Annie and Carlotta are somewhere down here."

The seven of us searched every room thoroughly in the hope of finding our friends but with no luck. As we turned down a corridor, we were met with more regulators and Uprising members locked in combat.

I dashed forward to help a young girl struggling against a much larger regulator who had her backed into the wall. Wrapping my arms around the regulator's neck, I pulled him backwards with all my might. Elliot punched his stomach while Kailey kicked out his shins. The girl lunged forward, striking the regulator with a punch below his jaw, which made him scream and race off.

"Wow, thank you all!" the girl squeaked before rushing to help another individual.

Elliot, Kailey, and I continued fighting side by side, helping those we could, while the rest of our group did the same. After a bit, it became evident that the Uprising was winning in this corridor. I sprinted with my group as they raced down another hall and began inspecting the rooms. Others in the Uprising did similar down other halls and corridors.

"Carlotta!" Chester cried out. I spun to follow his gaze, relief flooding over me as our leader emerged among the crowd. After shaking a regulator off her, she raced to the seven of us who instantly embraced her in a group hug. Her clothes were torn with dark, bloody stains. My heart sank as I noticed a scar on her ear and that her hearing aid was missing. I hugged her tightly, thankful to finally be reunited.

"Thank you all for coming," she breathed out, pulling on her ear and leaning close to each of us. "It's so wonderful to see all of you!" Her tone became more serious as she glanced us over. "Is everyone else safe? Did they take anyone else?"

"Annie!" Jennifer blurted out. "Please, have you seen her?"

"We'll find her. Come on!" Carlotta took Jennifer's hand as tears began forming in the twin's eyes. "Others are being freed down here. Annie might be among them."

We dashed down a corridor, moving as a tight-knit unit through the building.

"There's some of our people trapped in here!" A yell sounded above the noise, prompting those of us currently not fighting to turn to the source of the call. A girl struggled with a large door that had been locked with a chain. Before I could move, a sword slashed through the chain and the door broke open. People rushed out, cheerfully reuniting with their loved ones.

Annie! I peered over the crowd, hoping and praying to catch a glimpse of red hair among those that poured out the room. Jennifer rushed forward, crying out for her sister. As she and Carlotta returned to our side, I felt my stomach drop. *She's not here.* I shook away the regulator's remark that some had been killed. *Oh please, Lord! Let Annie be safe somewhere else in this building!*

My prayer was interrupted as loud bangs began to fill the space. *No, not again!* I shrieked, Elliot collapsing beside me. My ears rang and the world seemed to slow down as I crouched down next to my friend, his shirt turning red.

He lifted his head up slowly. "I'm so sorry," he muttered, spitting out blood.

"You didn't do anything wrong," I reassured Elliot as he laid his head back down against the hard floor, coughing up more blood. He began to inhale and exhale deeply and quickly. *God, no!* I thought, my heart sinking. *Please don't take him, please!*

I looked up as Max laid his hand on my shoulder. Not too far off lay Jennifer who was being comforted by Sid and Kailey. She gasped for air as she glanced around, presumably in the hope of spotting her sister among the crowd. My heart ached as blood poured out of her mouth. *She must have been shot, too . . .*

Directly behind them, Carlotta clung to Chester's body as tears streamed down her face. His eyes glanced at nothing and the light they once held was gone.

I tried to scream but nothing came out. Glancing back down at Elliot, I reached out and took his hand that now felt so heavy.

"You didn't do anything wrong," I repeated, my voice barely a whisper. "You did everything right. Everything you were supposed to. It's not your fault."

Elliot blinked up at me, his brown eyes pooling with water. I watched as his chest rose and fell, and his eyes started to focus on nothing. My own chest felt heavy, and I let out a shaky breath.

"Annie!" Max's voice cut through the ringing in my ears. Glancing up, I watched the twin appear within the crowd, racing to her sister's side. She came to a halt, standing over her twin for a few seconds before crashing to her knees and pulling Jennifer close to her in a hug. Jennifer wrapped her arms around Annie, grabbing her hand and squeezing it three times before going limp.

Cheers slowly cut through the ringing in my ears. I watched, feeling numb, as others in the Uprising raised green and orange flags. They shouted victory cries while they ran through the halls, chasing the regulators away.

"We won!" they hollered, drawing the battle to a close.

Did we? My tears spilled as Elliot's hand grew stiff and his eyes reflected nothing. I pulled him close while Max hugged the two of us tightly. I didn't feel like a winner right now and I felt certain others did not, either.

I watched Elliot's blood seep into the ground, a dizziness consuming me and stars clouding my vision. My efforts to blink it away failed as my eyes became worse. *Did we really win? Was the victory worth their lives?* Gasping for air, my vision turned black, and my body collapsed into Max's arms.

Chapter Forty

"It's called a family heirloom. At least, I believe that's the term our parents used before they passed. Of course, they had to hide it though."

I smiled as my triplet hooked the solid black cross necklace in place around my neck before patting my shoulders affectionately.

"Thanks Bennett," I said, giving him a quick hug. Finding him had been a lot easier than I had imagined. We had stumbled upon him one day during a trek into the city. He was pleasant and easy to get along with. Learning his story, and finding out he had fought against the regulators on the side of the Uprising during the final battle, gave me the biggest sense of relief. It was good to know that although he had been raised to be a regulator, it wasn't who he truly was on the inside. He was a good man, and I felt a sense of comfort whenever he was by my side.

Noise from the kitchen caused both of us to turn in that direction. I still resided in Elliot's old bedroom, as did Bennett. Although now the room felt more like an actual bedroom with new furniture.

"Are you two slowpokes coming, or what?" Annie asked, coming to a stop in the doorway. She placed a hand on her hip as she looked us over.

Bennett rolled his eyes, letting out a chuckle. "Well, we're ready, are you?" He handled her teenage sass well.

"Oliver's not!" Annie retorted as I slipped on my shoes.

"Am now!" I smiled, joining them at the door.

Annie let out a giggle, the three of us playfully bickering as we crossed the fully powered and stocked kitchen, quickly fled down the stairs, and joined the rest of the group at the back door.

***

I took a deep breath, following my friends into the woods. I was thankful for the change in weather in recent years. It was neither too hot nor too cold, but a comfortable temperature that made us all want to be outside. *It feels so perfect*, I thought before letting out a loud sneeze.

Kailey jumped, spinning around sharply to face me.

"Did I scare you?" I asked between fits of laughter.

"You wish, Oliver!" She giggled, turning back around. "I just wasn't expecting it."

"Oh, sure! Whatever you say."

I cast my gaze past her, picking up my pace as the pond came into view. I was eager to get there already and spend some time at the gravesites. Although nearly half a decade had passed since the Uprising took power during the Center City attack, my heart still ached for those we'd lost. I especially missed my dear friend Elliot. Our room felt so empty at times, even with Bennett around. Our late-night conversations helped, but nothing replaced the hole in my heart that Elliot and Olivia had left.

With the Uprising in charge, many changes had occurred through-out the city. For starters, my friends no longer had to hide their natural features. Regulators no longer terrorized the streets. Many of them assimilated quickly, as Bennett had done, pledging their loyalty to the Uprising and Harriet's rule as city governor. Some fled into the wilderness while other regulators followed in the footsteps of the emperor in taking their own lives, a shot he had fired into himself as the Uprising got closer and closer to his chamber in the final battle. We all slowly started to feel a bit safer and even Caleb could walk around the city in broad daylight without fear.

Our homes had gotten a bit of a makeover as well in recent years. The walls of our house had been reconstructed, we'd gotten some new furniture, and the side of our home had a beautiful butterfly mural done by Sid, who had become a popular artist with her murals throughout the city. She had also gained popularity by sharing some of her writing too. We were all deeply proud of her.

The city overall was striving to be less wasteful as people learned not only how to coexist with those who looked different or believed different, but also how to coexist with the environment in a sustainable way. Learning more about caring for the planet led many to contribute to the farm I knew so well. I had become a regular visitor over the years, watching it grow from a humble farm to massive fields full of vibrant plants. As more and more people helped Martha and the other farmers till the land, harvests were even more bountiful with plenty to share throughout the city. Martha became like a mother figure to me and Bennett, but I wished she could've been one to Olivia, too.

"We're nearly there!" Carlotta called from the lead. For the first few years after Chester's death, she had remained the sole leader of our group. Only very recently had she promoted Max to be her second in command, a decision I wholeheartedly supported. He trailed at her side now, conversing with Trevor as he helped the boy through some thick vegetation.

"That's so pretty!" Annie said, reaching through the vegetation for a wildflower. She plucked it with ease. "I'm going to give it to Jennifer."

I smiled. "She'll love that." I had left my own fair share of flowers at each of their graves, hoping the wind carried flowers to Olivia's grave as well. I had visited her burial site a few times, but it was definitely a hike to get there. Bennett had also joined me in trips to the pizzeria, which still stood abandoned. The two of us had decided to donate Olivia's clothes to give them a new life.

The grief of losing my sister still lingered from time to time, but I could now carry the heaviness with ease. I knew I had healed, as much as a person could from losing a sibling, the day I decided to bury her barrette in the ground next to her grave. Ever since that day, I walked with more of a spring in my step and with a heart that no longer felt so heavy.

I raced to the front of the group as we emerged into the clearing. The pond loomed straight ahead, its water a gorgeous blue with pink flowers covering most of the surface. Multiple lily pads had started to open up. The old truck stood frozen in time, covered by vegetation. The air around the pond smelled sweet, which I assumed was due to the blooming flowers.

I crossed the clearing and took a seat beside the pond. Carlotta came to sit next to me, adjusting her new hearing aid as Max and Trevor sat behind her. Trevor clung tightly to Max's arm as the two peered into the water. His smile warmed my heart. *Such a gentle soul with an excellent guide*, I thought, watching Trevor and Max as they gazed into the pond.

Kailey, Annie, and Sid raced around the truck to where we had buried our friends. Bennett followed them slowly. I watched as Annie placed the flower above the ground where we buried Jennifer. She had shown incredible strength since that day. I knew Jennifer would be proud of how far she'd come.

"We chose such a beautiful day to come here," Husker said as he took his spot beside us. The boy joined us on outings a lot more now since he no longer had to guard the house from regulators.

"Now that nature is starting to heal, we'll have plenty of days like this," Carlotta mentioned, gliding her hand across the water. She splashed some at us playfully. "I'm down to come back to this spot anytime you're up for the hike."

"Only if you promise to stop splashing us!" I joked, splashing some water in her direction as we all laughed. The water was cool, but not freezing.

She wiped her hand on her dress, looking amused. "Well, I don't know about that!"

"Then get used to getting splashed!" Max smirked, splashing some in her direction. Trevor and I jumped back, narrowly avoiding the water.

I stirred to my feet while my friends continued to tease one another. A butterfly landed close to me as I strolled past the rusting truck. The butterfly's green and black wings glowed in the sunlight, and I couldn't help but smile at the creature. We'd all been spotting butterflies in the days, months, and years since the deaths of Elliot, Chester, and Jennifer. Butterflies became an animal we associated them with and I also with Olivia. The sight of one instantly cheered us up with the hope our friends were safe and at peace elsewhere.

The butterfly flew off as I approached the graves. Alongside Jordyn's grave stood three new ones. The four graves were covered with flowers and knitted butterflies Carlotta had made. The girls and Bennett turned to greet me as I sat next to them at the foot of the graves. Bennett shifted close to me, and I laid my head gently on his shoulder.

"That flower looks beautiful there," I told Annie, who beamed at my words. Her flower bloomed despite being surrounded by decaying flowers. "I know Jennifer would appreciate that."

"Thank you!" she said, looking very pleased with herself.

"If you'd like to," Sid spoke up, "you can join us in searching through the woods for some fresh flowers to give Elliot and Chester and Jordyn. We were actually about to go do that."

I smiled. "I'd love to. Just give me a moment."

Sid nodded, the girls giving me and Bennett space as I pulled my head up from Bennett's shoulder and leaned closer to Elliot's grave.

"Take your time," Bennett whispered, stirring to his feet and joining the girls.

I remained silent, only nodding as I glanced over the ground. I felt a sense of comfort and warmth spread through my body. I missed my friend dearly and I also missed Olivia at times. I wished she too could have been buried here so I could visit both at the same time, but I knew both of them went with me everywhere I went. I could only hope I was making them proud as I strove to do my best every day.

I thought about Carlotta's words as another butterfly flew over us, causing the girls to cheerfully giggle and point at it. *Nature is healing, and so are we.* We had each been through so much, but still gave so much. These people had grown to mean the world to me, and I was thankful for the family I'd found in them. I was especially grateful each of them could exist as their true and authentic selves now that society was starting to heal too. The days of some no longer being considered worthy of inheriting the new earth were over. The city under Harriet's rule may not have all perfect people who looked the same, walked the same, or acted the same, but it sure had people who cared for one other, people who looked out for one another, and people who truly strove to love their neighbor. People who tried to make civilization a better place. And best of all, people who could now inherit this new earth regardless of who they were.

Happiness surged through me as I rose to my feet and followed the girls and Bennett to pick some flowers. No matter our circumstances, joy had made a permanent home with us. Nothing could break our spirits, and I felt the Holy Spirit wrap around me as I plucked a flower for Elliot. A peace unlike anything I'd ever experienced before entered me, causing me to smile from ear to ear.

No matter what the future throws our way, I thought. *We will manage just fine as a family.* Smelling the flower, I felt certain our future would be just as bright as the feeling that now surged through me.

Praise be to You always, Lord God!

Acknowledgements

I am eternally grateful for all who helped me in the journey of publishing my second book. To friends and family who encouraged me along the way, thank you. To all my readers, thank you. Your support is a driving force for my writing.

To my editor Gillian Rodgerson, thank you. I thoroughly appreciate the time and care you gave my manuscript. Thank you for helping me improve my story.

To my cover artist Driss Chaoui, thank you. You are brilliant and kind, and I can't wait to see how far you go with your art.

To the Parlier family, especially Mallory, thank you. Your support and feedback helped tremendously. I hope I've told Reed's story well.

To the One who knows me best, the Creator, Elohim, Lord God, thank you for everything. Thank you for the gift of life, and for every day you've blessed me with so I could complete and publish this book. Thank you for making a way and for never doubting even though I had plenty of doubts. Thank you for being my greatest friend and greatest ally. There will never be enough words to describe your love and goodness. I pray this work guides others to you, and I pray that you may continue to use me to bring you glory, for I am yours and all glory and honor is yours, forever and ever. I stand in awe of you, greatest author (Acts 3:15). I love you so.

And of course, to E. Reed Parlier and Riley C. Howell, thank you both. Your memories are a blessing that continue to strengthen and guide me daily. Reed, I hope you're happy with what I've done here. And Riley, I'm looking forward to writing your book. Anyone who knows me will know you all, too. See you both again when the time is right.

About the Author

Megan lives in Charlotte, North Carolina. Born and raised in Louisville, Kentucky, she moved to North Carolina to complete degrees at the University of North Carolina at Charlotte and Duke University, where she completed her bachelor's and master's degrees (respectively). She is also the author of *The Bible is Not an Anti-Gay Weapon* and plans to publish more books in the future. To learn more about Megan and her books, visit www.meganbeachauthor.com